LOBO GRAY

LOBO GRAY

L. L. FOREMAN

WHEELER
CHIVERS

This Large Print edition is published by Wheeler Publishing, Waterville, Maine USA and by BBC Audiobooks Ltd, Bath, England.
Wheeler Publishing is an imprint of Thomson Gale, a part of The Thomson Corporation.
Wheeler is a trademark and used herein under license.

LIBRARY OF CONGRESS CATALOGING-IN-PUBLICATION DATA

Foreman, L. L. (Leonard London), 1901–
  Lobo gray / by L. L. Foreman.
    p. cm. — (Wheeler Publishing large print westerns)
  ISBN 1-59722-338-7 (lg. print : pbk. : alk. paper)
    1. Large type books. I. Title. II. Series: Wheeler large print western series.
PS3511.O427L63 2006
813'.54—dc22
                                                2006019468

BRITISH LIBRARY CATALOGUING-IN-PUBLICATION DATA AVAILABLE

Published in 2006 in the U.S. by arrangement with Golden West Literary Agency.
Published in 2007 in the U.K. by arrangement with Golden West Literary Agency.

U.K. Hardcover: 978 1 405 63938 5 (Chivers Large Print)
U.K. Softcover: 978 1 405 63939 2 (Camden Large Print)

Printed in the United States of America on permanent paper.
10 9 8 7 6 5 4 3 2 1

LOBO GRAY

1
"CALL ME LOBO"

He came like a hard-used lance from many battles, the scars and nicks worn smooth on the close-grained timber, the tempered steel blade bright and sharp. Upon certain kinds of men, his appearance had much the same challenging effect as that of a strange warrior upon a camp of Comanche bucks. And that was the effect he had upon the fighting men of Blakeville, the town he hit last in his drift up through the Territory.

Blakeville was not the official name of the town. It had come to be called that at first in irony and later by common custom. A heavy proportion of its male citizens owed a kind of loyalty to the name and what it stood for, and being bound thereby to assert their dominance over all others outside their ring, they promptly bristled at this stranger whose very bearing constituted a challenge.

They took note of his lean Spanish gun,

as well as of a couple of other below-the-border touches about him, and were led to surmise that he might be part Mexican. He wasn't, but the rumor fed their urge to lay him out. The urge gathered like a thickening odor, smelled by him everywhere he turned.

He could have avoided the issue by drifting on quietly after dark, without loss to his ego, for he was not a man who was easily lured into senseless gunplay. But he had begun seeing possibilities for himself in Blakeville. He chose to stay.

The first man he clashed with was Jack Shears, who ran the games in the Bullhead Bar, a dangerous occupation in such a town, requiring among other gifts a talent for homicide. Jack Shears had the talent.

Jack Shears also had a woman, a sultry lulu with the unlikely name of Platonita. In discussing the stranger with her man, Platonita let drop an unguarded remark. The stranger, she said, struck her as somebody special. "His eyes kind of wrap you up in one look. I bet he can set a woman on fire and keep her faithful. Know what I mean, Jack?"

Watching the expression on her ivory face as she talked of the stranger in town, Jack Shears nodded soberly.

"He's not Mexican," she said positively. "I bet there's not a drop of Mexican blood in him."

"Pretty soon," the gambler murmured, "we'll find out the color of his blood. . . ." Then he slapped her in the face.

He led the play that night over a poker table in the Bullhead. Without any preliminaries, he called the stranger a foul name while stroking hand to holster. Platonita was there, as were all others having foreknowledge of Shears' intention and interest in the outcome. The thing was rigged, odds in favor of the gambler.

An instant after he spoke, Jack Shears crumpled, a bullet through his head. A man to one side of him, who later claimed to have reached only for a handkerchief, blinked sickly down at a broken arm. On Shears' other side, a standing man swayed into the table, and the dealer skidded backward in his chair before it slewed around and threw him.

He who held the Spanish gun then stood quite still, his forearm rigid along his ribs, the weapon jutting straight. During the shattering roar, he had twisted his body left and right, faster than a sparring boxer. None of the men he shot had even so much as finished unsheathing a weapon; their mo-

9

tions were canceled in that instant between grip and draw. The terrible efficiency of it stunned the onlookers to dead silence.

Platonita took a faltering step forward and froze, staring at him. "You — you!" — she whispered, then reverted to her native tongue. — "*lobo!* Who are you? Tell me, so I shall know the name to curse! Tell me!"

He laid his glance on her and considered the question while she shriveled under what she took to be the cold cruelty in his agate eyes. "All right," he said at last. "Call me Lobo." As an afterthought he added, "Gray."

That was how Lobo Gray came to the notice of Judge Blake, by cool intention. Judge Blake, first citizen of Blakeville, was the law, and his influence reached far beyond the town; his fame was rising and his name seemed likely to shine as that of a patriotic champion of progress, a political organizer on what many people still loosely called the frontier.

The charge was murder.

It was a ripe time for champions of progress. The early adventurers and soldiers of fortune, Spanish *conquistadores*, American trappers and Indian-fighters — the whole trail-breaking lot of them had ended their day and passed on. There had been an exhausting internecine war, followed by an influx of restless newcomers, most of them accustomed to the use of arms, many of them at odds with the law.

Because of its geography and the times, the Territory drew more than its share of the lawless. High mountain fastnesses lay on the north, and to the south trackless deserts and convenient proximity to Old Mexico. Between, there were great stretches of rich land, of uncertain ownership ever since the Mexican War had plunged the old Spanish land grants into legal chaos. There was a pervading go-to-hell air of instability in which men felt free to live like savages if they wished.

Certainly it was the time for champions of progress to rise and till the unruly field, and so they did. Among them were some who sowed the seeds of pioneer politics and others who reaped harvests for themselves. Anthony Blake did both. He was said to be of a prominent New England family. It was also rumored that he was the leader of the conspirators who for profit had contrived the betrayal of Crabb's Expedition into Sonora in '57.

Whatever his background, he was able to exert some influence in Washington, winning appointment as district judge when he needed it to enforce his spreading control over the Lower Pecos Valley.

To the valley ranches, formerly operated in slapdash, independent fashion, he brought progressive measures that usually eventuated in a transfer of ownership — to him. The ranches were mostly small, held on flimsy proof of title, but in the aggregate they formed an immense terrain extending clear down to the Rio Grande. For the rancher who didn't care to co-operate, the alternative was a court order from Blakeville, the Judge's headquarters, served by armed men who might or might not escort him back alive to argue his case.

The Upper Pecos was something else. Perhaps the high country bred men of sharper edge, men more cantankerous and prickly than those of the hot lowlands. For one thing, they had more room, were less prone to the cautioning advice of neighbors. The Judge realized that it would be no easy task to spread his holdings on up into the mountains, where grass was not the problem that it was down in the valley when rain failed and the Pecos ran dry.

Meantime, the Lower Pecos required constant policing by men swift to stamp out any spark of rebellion. Unending vigilance was the price paid by a leader who aspired to greatness. He was always in the market for outstanding gunfighters.

The Judge hired Lobo Gray.

"You'll carry your gun for me, or you'll hang!" he stated flatly in the privacy of his office.

Lobo Gray nodded, unsurprised. "We're starting out on the right foot. I'm never friends with the man who hires me."

The Judge gazed at him, wondering if jail wouldn't be best. But a bad condition existed in Blakeville, because of the type of men he employed. The large number of hard cases posed the inevitable difficulty of keeping them from fighting among themselves. He was in the position of an owner of savage dogs, all striving to lead the pack, flying at one another's throats as soon as their master turned his back. Yet he had to maintain the pack at hand, ready to draw upon as immediate necessity rose.

Blakeville was earning a steadily worsening reputation far and wide as the toughest town in the Territory — his own town, his headquarters. And he had come to the time when he needed to purify his name, polish his halo, and conceal the ugliness underlying his rising career.

In Lobo Gray's look and manner the Judge perceived a thorny spirit, strangely reckless. Something about the man disturbed him. His look warned that he would kick aside any authority set over him, laugh in the face of death, spit in the devil's eye. Acting on a premonition that Lobo Gray was potentially too dangerous to remain alive, the Judge handed him the suicidal job of policing Blakeville. He hardly thought Gray would take it on as he said, "I *can* sentence you to hang, if you want to know!"

What he received in return was a challenging glance and the dry question: "Did I ask you?"

In short order Gray gave the troublemakers lethal proof that he would finish whatever shooting was started in the town. He had a curious, difficult gun trick of clamping his forearm against his ribs, after a lightning draw, and pivoting his body to bring the gun dead on the mark every time. Few men could master this maneuver with any high degree of speed and accuracy. It was a technique designed primarily for use against two or more opponents — from which the Judge shrewdly observed that Gray was by inclination and training a lone wolf, a gunfighter who placed his faith in himself and nobody else.

Later, the Judge found reason to add that

Gray was not friendly to anybody, didn't even seem to like himself. A lonely man, this Lobo Gray, an unhappy man, driven into violence by secret reasons of his own.

His age was about thirty, but often he looked much older. At rare times, when the bleakness happened to lift from his agate eyes, he looked younger. He was built large, though lean as a wolfhound, and he had the ridged brows and scarred face of a scrapper who had taken his batterings in many a wicked fight.

The Judge never quite relinquished his first impression of Lobo Gray. But he came to value him highly. Finally he promoted him to the top, there being no other man in the crew anywhere nearly as well-qualified to fill it, nor any man willing to take it over Gray's head.

"I'll give you the orders," the Judge told Gray, "and it will be your responsibility to see that they're carried out. You'll be in command of the enforcers."

By "enforcers" he meant his crew of hard cases, ostensibly a standing posse. Since embarking upon his campaign to clean up his reputation for political purposes, it had become his habit to employ lofty euphemisms in place of plain speech, and that one brought a faint twitch of irony to Gray's lips.

Gray nodded a casual acceptance. By then he was the acknowledged top dog of the Blakeville pack anyway, and he regarded this promotion simply as the Judge's formal recognition of the fact. He had taken to wearing two guns, both of which he was able to use with equally devastating proficiency.

"A good foreman, with nerve and initiative and a very close mouth, is hard to find," the Judge began.

"Ramrod," Gray murmured. "Gun boss."

The Judge raised his bald, ponderous head, frowning, a chill displeasure lurking in his pale eyes. But he allowed the correction to pass and spoke of pay.

"I shall expect you to earn it. As my own duties and activities increase, I must rely more and more on you to handle the outside details. There can be no pause in progress, as Goethe said. It places many burdens on my shoulders."

This time, Gray grinned openly. Duties and activities. Progress. The Judge, climbing into notice as a land-and-cattle baron and a political power, seeing himself as a rising man of destiny, could no longer afford the risk of personally directing a crew of thugs.

"I'll handle 'em," Gray said.

He left without waiting for the Judge's gesture of dismissal, without offering a word of thanks for the promotion. The Judge, as he had done months before, stared after him, narrow-eyed, knowing him no better now than he had then, remembering that Gray had said he was never friends with the man who hired him.

Leaving the Judge's house, Gray thought: "Gun boss of Blakeville. . . ."

He had set out from the first day to win the job, having sized up the layout and foreseen the Judge's need for a lieutenant to run the crew. Because of its obstacles, the goal had sustained him with a kind of dour zest. It had kept him occupied, kept his faculties warily alert and his wits honed sharp. It was a game to fill the vacuum in his life.

And now that he had won it, he couldn't feel a particle of excitement over it. Instead, he felt let down, as though he had come to a dead end. He tried to account for his depression by laying it to a lack of ambition, an underlying reluctance to take on responsibility. Deep within himself, he knew better.

Half angrily, he told himself, "What more could you want? The mighty Judge Blake's ramrod! Lord! That's about as high as any gunslinger can go. This time I'll stick with it. This time. . . ."

Already the black imps were beginning ever so slightly to stir at the back of his mind; the perverse black imps that had betrayed him before and destroyed his hard-won eminence in other regions where the fastest gun carried the crown. If they betrayed him here, he foresaw it would be for the last time. The job of carrying out the Judge's orders entailed gaining knowledge of the Judge's secrets. No man possessing such dangerous knowledge could expect to kick over the traces and stay alive.

"This time I'm in for keeps!" Gray muttered, and having so decided in this moment of cold reason, he strode on in the baking afternoon heat to inform the Judge's enforcers that they had a permanent ram-rod.

He trod the dusty main street to the west side on foot — these days he seldom took his horse out of the livery stable, preferring to walk about town unhampered in case of sudden flare-ups and the ever-likely possibility of somebody's emptying a gun at him as a tempting target. Cowpunchers commonly saddled up to travel a couple of hundred yards, but a man in his trade could pay with his life for the luxury of riding

18

down a street.

As he stepped up onto the boardwalk, he glimpsed in the corner of his eye a woman on the other side of the street, emerging from the emporium next door to Paley's Palace. He jerked his head around and stopped short with a strangled grunt, his eyes widening. The woman had a slender body, young and willowy. She wore a hooded bonnet against the fierce sun and held her head bent so that Gray saw only the lower part of her profile and a curl of raven hair. Evidently sensing his fixed stare, she turned her face fully toward him, smiling readily.

A painted face.

Seeing the brightness drain abruptly from his eyes, the woman shrugged and walked on into Paley's Palace. A new woman, or one he hadn't noticed before. A fleeting trick of sunlight and shadow, that was all. She was not the woman he had for a few mad seconds imagined her to be — not a bit like her.

He went on his way, brows drawn and mouth set cruelly hard.

The black imps stirred.

2
LOBO MEANS WOLF

The batwing doors flapped, and over his drink Lobo Gray watched Bas Tomayo, a new man, come into the Bullhead Bar with a written notice in his hand. Gray finished his drink thoughtfully. He was not drunk, but he had arrived at the stage where a sardonic humor tugged at him. He snapped his empty glass to the table, and at the click of it the whole barroom, already subdued, grew absolutely quiet. Glances cut to him and slid off.

He was familiar with the contents of the written notice in Bas Tomayo's brown hand. Copies of it were being posted up today all over Blakeville. It concerned him, was aimed directly at him, and everybody in town knew it.

After two years as ramrod, riding high, he had fallen out of favor for the final time, and now the Judge was cracking down on him. The notice might just as well have proclaimed open season on Lobo Gray.

He had done much for the Judge these two past years, had served him well and won his praise. But the black imps could not always be denied, and when they clamored and clawed in him, he sought release and found trouble. He made trouble, kicked it up, and then slammed it down. Drinking made him utterly unpredictable. He could control the crew, but in those spells he could not govern himself, and he taunted them and fought with them, fist and gun, ugly fights, hating the sight of them. A deep weariness was growing within him. His outbursts had become increasingly frequent. He earned his high pay and spent it, flung it away, a town-tamer gone wild. Often, lately, he woke up with blood on him and no clear recollection of how it had got there.

But he was not drunk now, not yet, and he watched with saturnine interest as Bas Tomayo picked a prominent spot on the barroom wall on which to post the notice.

Bas Tomayo tacked the notice up, using the butt of his gun as a hammer. Although he had fire-red hair and yellow eyes, and had ridden into Blakeville from the north, Bas Tomayo's dark skin bespoke a strong Mexican strain. He was small, neatly dressed, a trim little man of uncertain age who might have passed unregarded if nature had spared him that hybrid blend of coloration. As it was, his flaming hair was the target of jibes that were caustic because the men disliked the feline quality of his eyes

21

and scorned his dark skin and small size.

He turned from tacking up the notice to find Gray towering over him. Gray said, "You've been trailing me all round town with those things. Judge's orders, or your own idea?"

Bas Tomayo smiled politely, shaking his head. In his broken English he answered, "Judge, he say put up papers all place." He shrugged. "I put up."

"How many more you got?"

"Is the last."

"Good. Hope you liked the work."

"Gracias."

Bas Tomayo departed, and Gray scanned the notice to see if it was the same as the others. It was, down to Judge Blake's signature. Its wording was plain:

Warning!

Henceforth, be it known that when death is caused by the violent act of any person known to have committed a similar act previously in this district, the plea of self-defense will not be accepted in my court. The charge shall be Murder, fully prosecuted. *There shall be no exception made.*

And that, Gray mused, put him flat on

the spot. With these words the Judge had opened the door wide for everybody to take a crack at him, once they had thoroughly digested the novel thought that they could now do so with impunity. There wasn't a man in the crew who wouldn't relish baiting him, daring him to pull a gun. *There shall be no exception made.* . . . One shot and he was finished. They'd gamble that he would not draw and fire that fatal shot.

So the Judge had decided that his gun boss was becoming too dangerous, too unruly, had he? Throwing him to the wolves. Opening the field for a new ramrod, one that might prove to be more controllable. Well, maybe the Judge was right, Gray inwardly conceded, but damned if he was going to submit to the sacrifice.

Stepping away from the notice on the wall, he wheeled quickly and met the eyes of another new man — Bert Ernst, a gunman supposedly from Texas and reputed to have a string of killings behind him. Ernst, as soon as he arrived in town, had called respectfully on the Judge. During the three days since, he had circulated around and struck up acquaintance with most of the crew. Like Bas Tomayo, today he was cropping up wherever Gray went, touring the bars. In Tomayo's case it was fairly explainable, but something more than coincidence lay behind Ernst's appearances.

Meeting his stare in that fleeting instant, Gray knew beyond a doubt that Ernst was stalking him with deadly purpose.

It had been many moons since Gray had been on the receiving end of a manhunt. To find himself filling the role now gave him an odd sense of exhilaration, above the challenge of it. The challenge was real, and the dice were loaded against him. On the one hand, a shoot-out would put his neck in the noose; on the other, Bert Ernst was prepared to shoot for the top job.

The Texas killer had spent his three days in Blakeville gainfully, asking the crew questions about him, learning the details of his gun technique. He'd had time to study him, to devise a counter-technique of his own, and he was ready, waiting only for the right chance. Gray, who made his own chances as he went along, measured Ernst as a careful man, one with the planning mind of a professional assassin. Ernst and the Judge would get along well, each understanding the workings of the other's mind.

Along with an urge to do mischief, a degree of caution rose to ballast Gray's mood, and he moved slowly in among the gambling tables, glancing at the sets of players as if choosing his game. Ernst, standing with his back to the bar and studying him closely, allowed a flicker of interest to cross his sharp, narrow face when Gray struck his knuckles clumsily against the edge of a poker table.

Gray chose that table. He dragged out a chair and sank heavily into it, rubbing his knuckles. The four men playing there kept their eyes down.

"Deal me in."

The game was stud. Without looking at his hole card, Gray stayed with the betting and raised it the third time around. His chair faced away from the bar, but by the stillness of the other players, he knew when Ernst came soundlessly up behind him.

"Any man who'd bet blind on a jack high card against aces showing," drawled the Texas gunman, "is either drunk or a natural-born muttonhead — likely both!"

Gray had his hands flat before him on the table, elbows resting on the arms of his chair. He asked, not turning his head, "Who says so?"

"Me. Bert Ernst!"

"Move 'round front of me and say it again!"

"The move's yours, you lousy bluffer . . . if you got the guts!"

25

Gray turned his head then, just far enough to see that Ernst was standing close over him, crowding him. Ernst was taking care to cramp his style, leaving no room for him to take stance and get his gun technique into action.

Ernst's eyes held a dull glow of intentness. He was out to make his kill, had committed himself irretrievably to it. All he waited for was a move on Gray's part, any kind of move that could be construed as an attempted draw, to give credence later to the gunman's brag that he had outshot Gray.

"How did a false alarm like you ever get to ride so high?" he jeered.

Cold sober, Gray said almost mildly, "Let me show you," and pushed back his chair.

His body blocking the chair as it came to him, Ernst laid hand to holster, ready to meet Gray's rise and turn with an instant blast. But Gray remained seated, although his hands shifted onto the arms of his chair, and Ernst made to speak again.

Gray brought one leg up, jackknifed, and hooked his bootheel onto the edge of the table. He snapped his leg straight, fast. The table skidded until it rammed into the other seated players, while the back of Gray's chair drove hard into Ernst's stomach. Ernst grunted, giving way a stumbling step. Gray spun to his feet with room to spare for action.

Gray still left his guns holstered. He had led Ernst on, offered him a tempting opportunity to disclose his murderous intention, and Ernst had fallen for it. The point was not to kill Ernst but to break and degrade him in the eyes of the crew. Gray lunged at him. His open hand caught the killer a fearful smack full in the face.

Rattled, his close calculations gone to pot, Ernst backstepped to recover balance. Another smack, and he fumbled his draw. He was trying to dodge at the same time, amazed and confused by Gray's unorthodox tactics. Gray reached back, grasped his chair with one hand, and flung it at him. It smashed into Ernst and carried him to the floor.

Gray kicked the chair aside and stood over him. He stamped his foot on Ernst's half-drawn gun and scraped it clear. Ernst stared dazedly up at him and raised an arm in futile defense. Gray reached down, yanked him onto his feet, and without speaking propelled him across the barroom. Ernst's feet dragged. Within a stride of the doors, Gray dropped back, shot his boot out, and kicked Ernst through the doors head first.

Gray looked around. The men grinned. Few of the grins were genuine, but nobody present was about to take up for a loser. Gray walked back to the poker table, where he proceeded to show proof that his card sense was as sharp as ever.

"Judge Blake say you come to him *muy pronto, señor.*"

It was Bas Tomayo who brought the peremptory order, delivering it in a respectful tone while halting several paces from the poker table. Raking in his fourth straight pot, Gray stacked coins and nodded to the dealer.

"Muy pronto," Tomayo repeated.

"Tell him I'll be along," Gray said, and the listening men in the barroom sent him hard looks. Any summons from the Judge carried the implicit command that a man drop everything and jump to it. To flout it was to break the first rule of discipline, a discipline that Gray himself had imposed upon the Judge's henchmen.

"Is *importante,*" Tomayo murmured.

"So's this," Gray said. But the other players threw in their cards, and with a shrug he quit the game. Bas Tomayo was edging toward the bar, as diffident in manner as a lad doubting his rights among men. Gray flipped a silver dollar over to a bartender and called, "His drink's on me."

Bas Tomayo stopped dead. For an instant his eyes reflected surprise, almost a look of confusion, before he continued his course to the bar, where the bartender was sliding forward bottle and glass.

Nobody, Gray guessed, had bought Tomayo a drink since he had come to Blakeville. The little man was unpopular, and he kept to himself. Still, that was a queer look. . . .

The thought was swept from his mind as Gray caught a different kind of look in the eyes of two men standing by the front window. They were two men with whom Bert Ernst had been particularly friendly. Gazing out through the window, they turned their heads slightly and shot sidelong looks at Gray as he reached the batwing doors abreast of them. Blankness masked their eyes, meeting his, but there remained an impression of glittering expectation . . . Gray knew for a cold certainty that Bert Ernst had got hold of another gun and was waiting somewhere outside to cut him down.

He stood regarding the doors before him, while with dispassionate deduction his mind searched out Ernst's whereabouts. The Bullhead hitchrack, with four or five horses tied up to it, stood somewhat out of line with the doors. Ernst would not take that obvious spot as his station. Too risky; if he wasted his first shot and spooked the horses, he'd be a dead duck, no second chance.

No. Bert Ernst had more sense. A single shot, carefully sighted, without warning and with the least risk, would be the way of his kind. The way of a killer. Mr. Ernst would not be on this side of the street at all. He'd be crouched on the other side, employing cover and probably a gun rest, nursing his desire for revenge and his ambition as avid contender for the ramrod position due to become vacant.

The other side of the street, then, not too far off, and more or less facing the Bullhead — that was the ticket. Gray eliminated the emporium. Its proprietor, a crusty Scotsman, would never allow his establishment to fall into bushwhack use if he could help it. Paley's Palace was the logical spot. Gray didn't get on well with Paley.

He moved a little nearer to the doors and looked out over their curve-cut tops. No bullet came. Here in shadow he was not visible to anyone across the street, or at least not visible enough to recognize. On the other hand, Ernst enjoyed the same advantage, if he was in Paley's Palace. The entrance there was wide open, but in the murky interior nothing could be seen, not a movement. Ernst was playing it safe.

Furthermore, Ernst would want to be positive that it was Gray emerging from the Bullhead, would even want to know a second or two ahead of time, so as to avoid any possibility of a slip. Gray shot a glance at the two men at the window alongside him. Their faces were stamped with unbearable suspense, and one of the pair had halted his hand midway in the sly act of touching the window.

"I'm buying the drinks," Gray told them. "Get up to the bar."

They sucked air softly through closed teeth, backing slowly to the bar, and Gray moved over to the window. He placed his hand flat against the grimy pane, and wigwagged it, watching Paley's Palace.

Promptly on the signal, a figure darted forward from the dim interior of Paley's Palace into the lighter shadow of the entrance. There it crouched down on one knee, head cocked over a leveled rifle. It was Bert Ernst, and he held the rifle sighted man-high at the doors of the Bullhead Bar, waiting to squeeze the trigger on Gray.

Gray let him wait a brief spell, to ravel his nerves, to make him shoot too soon. This,

31

the foresighted figuring, and the juggling with fractions of time were the habitual result of his own discipline. Some flaming day he would forget it, he supposed, or cast it off. Blind rage, overconfidence, hot pride — down he would go, like so many other gunslingers he had seen and known. No; not pride. He was not proud of what he was.

He shifted to the doors, saying loudly, drunkenly, "Damn it, me in a winning streak and the Judge sends for me! Wouldn't you know!" He kicked the doors and sprang back to the window.

The rifle cracked. A neat round hole dotted an upper panel of the right-hand door, and the bullet ripped on high into the backbar. An ornamental tier of glasses collapsed and rained down in a musical cascade, accompanying the cursing of the pelted bartender below. Ernst must have heard that, for he jumped up in frantic haste. He couldn't know whether he had missed with his premature shot or scored a through-and-through hit, and it left him undecided between fleeing and staying. He levered a fresh shell into the breech of the heavy rifle.

Gray resolved his problem for him. He wrecked the window with a slash of his drawn gun, fired once, and watched Ernst come lurching involuntarily out into the sunshine. Ernst dropped to one knee again in the beginning of a fall. Gray hoped that the one crippling shot would suffice to make the man call it a day.

Gray stepped out of the Bullhead Bar. He called, "Ernst, have you had enough?" But he saw his hope going. The wounded gunman, crazed with pain and defeat, pushed the rifle forward and got it raised.

Gray fired his second shot. The flat, sullen echo of the report dissolved along the empty street, and during the moment of silence he heard Snuffy Locke, an Australian bruiser, exclaim in the barroom behind him, "Gawd! I've seen some bad bloody wolves in my time! . . ."

And then the soft voice of little Bas Tomayo: "*Lobo* means wolf . . ."

The aftermath hit Gray with a sick disgust. He ranged a bleak stare up and down the main street, mentally cursing Blakeville, the Judge and all his bailiwick, and himself. One more rabid fool beaten, lying dead over there in front of Paley's Palace for the town to bury. They never would learn, and he never would be able to avoid them. The higher a gunhawk flew, the more such fools he had to contend with; the longer he lived by maintaining his reputation, the harder they tried to bring him down. This was why he had turned to drink and trouble, but he was sick of that, too. He'd had enough.

Two years, he had lasted here. He shook his head. Odd, his lasting that long. He laid it to some kind of purposeless fluke of fate, for he had not paid too much care to staying alive, especially of late. His time was about up now, though.

His gaze stopped at the familiar white house on the low hill overlooking the town. An imposing house, containing courtroom and office and spacious living quarters, built to the Judge's specifications and paid for by allegedly grateful citizens of the district. The Judge, he remembered, had sent for him.

Or had he? The message delivered to him by Bas Tomayo could have been a fake, cooked up to tool him out of the Bullhead and straight into Bert Ernst's rifle fire . . . Bas Tomayo, the two men at the barroom window, and Ernst lying in wait. *Muy pronto. Importante.* Gray uttered a short laugh and struck off up the street toward the Judge's white house.

"Well, he'll sure want to see me now, if he didn't before!"

The Judge would be frigidly angry, his edict broken on the very day he issued it, by the man at whom it was aimed. As he mounted the steps to the big house, Gray wondered if the Judge's anger could ever be heated and made to explode. It would bring on a blazing finish for the man who did it — that or the thousand-to-one chance of coming out on top. The Judge, having his own special tricks and vast resources, had never yet failed to annihilate anyone opposing him; but there was generally a first time for everything.

Gray considered trying the experiment.

At the front door one of the house guards, ever present, nodded woodenly to Gray. "He's in the office," he said, moving aside from the small hall table where all callers were required to check their guns.

"Hunnh," Gray acknowledged, passing by and leaving the table bare, breaking another strict rule. The armed guard didn't attempt to halt him, but he stepped quickly back to the open door, and Gray heard him whistle.

Wearing his guns, Gray walked into the Judge's office.

3
LOBO AT LARGE

The Judge sat behind his desk, reading a letter. He did not look up or speak, and without invitation Gray hooked a straight-back chair around with his toe and seated himself where he could keep an eye on the office door.

"You sent for me?"

Intentionally, Gray let his query drag out, stripped of respect. Once he had been his own man, his own master, beholden to nobody. Often he remembered it, as he did now, and with the memory came crowding the pictures of the things that had happened since. To change that pattern of thought, he considered what the result would be if he were to tell the Judge to his face, right now, his plain opinion of him.

The Judge would listen gravely. In rebuttal he would state that his methods were vindicated by his objective — progress — and that the end justified the means. He would thoroughly believe it himself, too. And between two words he'd pull some diabolical trick, blindingly fast and merciless. . . . The next day, shaking his head sadly at the funeral, he'd say:

"Very regrettable. He was a good man." A sigh. "I shall miss him. However, there was nothing else to do. He went mad, like a dog. When a dog, even the most valuable, turns on you — well, it has to be killed. Regrettable, though."

Gray's lips twitched in satirical amusement. He had seen the Judge play that little act a time or two, and he had caught a grain of grim humor in it. The Judge could never admit that any henchman of his might flare up in rebellion against him. To his nerveless intelligence such behavior was irrational. It signified madness. Therefore, any man who attempted to cross him was mad and had to be killed. His policy of necessity included decent burial and a few kind words of eulogy containing a hint of warning to anybody else who might feel an urge to blow his cork. The Judge had a taste for ceremony when it served a purpose.

The huge desk, littered untidily as always with stacks of papers and cigar ash, had sliding drawers built on it, topped by a row of open pigeonholes. From behind it the Judge looked at Gray with a fixed, unblinking stare. He must have noticed Gray's guns immediately, for nothing ever escaped his eyes, but he passed no comment on them.

Without taking his stare off Gray, he reached forward, plucked a cigar from the open drawer where he kept them, and, leaning back, lighted it carefully. The oversize swivel chair creaked under his weight, and that was the only sound for a moment.

Gray thought, *Now I'll tell him! Now!*

But he felt himself growing smaller. He

had taken his orders so often in this room, from this man. The knowledge struck him that his long service to the Judge had ingrained in him a consciousness of subordination and rendered him scarcely fit for much else. It was he who, outwardly unmoved, broke the locked glance.

Yet he knew, better than anyone else, what kind of man the Judge was. He had seen the cynical hypocrisy beneath the virtuous halo, the utterly unscrupulous machinations of the cunning brain, the ruthless ambition that readily employed sinister trickery, shameful treachery, and appalling brutality. He also knew of secret vices of such black depths as to rot the character of any normal man.

The Judge was anything but normal, mentally or physically, and spiritually he didn't exist. He had the overwhelming manner and appearance of greatness, so rare in the truly great. An immense body, the hairless head so nobly proportioned that it seemed exaggerated, as if fashioned by a sculptor with a bent toward caricature.

At last he spoke, lowering his gaze to the letter. "I heard shots in town. Three."

In his mind, Gray reviewed the notices tacked up by Bas Tomayo. No exceptions. *Meaning me!* Anger tightened the skin beneath his eyes. A trap had been laid for him. He heard the footsteps of house guards outside the office door, and he thought, *Here goes.*

He said, "Two of the shots were mine. That new gun wonder of yours finally got round to showing his stuff. You'll have to pick a better man. His stuff was no good."

The Judge looked up without raising his great shining head. It always came as something of a minor shock to meet those staring, metallic eyes, pale like unblued gunmetal, with the same dull sheen. He looked into Gray's face, saw something there besides the scar-ravaged features, and slowly leaned forward in his chair.

"If you mean Ernst," he said calmly, "nobody picked him. He drifted in and asked my permission to stay a while."

"He'll stay a long while!"

"You killed him, in spite of —"

"On my second shot. My first didn't satisfy him."

"Hmm." The pale gaze dipped briefly to Gray's hands. A slight frown furrowed the sweeping brow. "An extenuating circumstance? Self-defense? I remind you that my order —"

Gray stood up. The Judge scanned his face again, and this time dropped the glance to his cigar. Distinctly, for the ears of the house guards, Gray said, "Any man pulling iron on me is a dead duck, to hell with your order! No exceptions!"

The Judge suddenly smiled. "Man, you're cocked!" he chided. "This attitude of yours is all wrong. I've known men in your mood to go berserk. What's making you so edgy, so difficult to handle these days? You've been with me two years now, long enough for you to know —"

"Too long," Gray cut in. "I'm sick of it. And damn sick of you, for that matter! Now call in the help and let's get this over!"

"Drop it!" said the Judge. "I wouldn't call in help if I wanted you out of the way. What's got into you? Haven't I given you authority second only to my own? Paid you well? Made you privy to my confidential activities?"

"Privy?" Gray snorted a laugh. "Whatever meaning you give to that word. I know what it stands for where I come from. Your confidential activities stink! I'm through!"

"Conscience?" The Judge pronounced it with an inflection of disbelief. "My God! The shackles of the weak and timid! Something that never burdened me."

"You lack other things, too."

"That's probably the secret of my success,

Gray. You must lack all conscience and sentiment if you wish to be successful. Gray, look at me. There's a strong movement afoot to gain statehood for the Territory. I shall be its first governor! After that, who knows? I hold more power in this country than the government at Washington!"

"In your own bailiwick," Gray corrected dryly. "That's big, but it doesn't cover the whole Territory."

"It will," the Judge promised. "It will! And that's progress. When I first came here it was a no man's land, people at odds with one another over water and range rights, settling their differences without recourse to law. Cattlemen had no idea of co-operative marketing. No system. There was no political organization. In time I changed all that. Progress!"

"At a hell of a price to the cattlemen!"

"Progress!" repeated the Judge. "Naturally, when order is imposed, those who resist it incur penalties. Sit down." He tapped a finger on the open letter before him. "I have a piece of business to discuss with you. It may take your mind off your mad delusions."

"Another confidential activity? I've told you —"

"Sit down! This concerns the Upper Pecos."

Gray remained standing, shuttling his glance between the desk and the door. But the showdown stage had passed, he gauged. His deliberate prodding had failed to stir up a storm, and the Judge for some reason was choosing to take an inconclusive course in the matter of the shooting of Ernst. Seeking the cause, Gray asked a question:

"Do you aim to make another try at moving in on the Upper Pecos range?"

"I've never given up trying," the Judge answered. "You know a lot about me, Gray, but not everything. My aim there has not changed, but my mistake lay in my approach. Yes, even I can make a mistake. I should have struck early and hard. Instead, I went at it patiently. I was engaged in other affairs and couldn't spare the Upper Pecos the benefit of my undivided effort, you see. And now some of the cowmen up there have taken advantage of my patience by banding against me. They've formed a sort of wildcat company. You've heard of it."

The pseudorighteous eloquence and splashes of pomposity provoked in Gray a tired irritation. He shrugged. "The Sierra Verde Pool — everybody's heard of it. Not a company. Just a pool of cowfolks who

42

figure they can protect their interests better by throwing in together. Maybe they can. Maybe you're trying to bite off more'n you can chew."

"Is that what you think?"

Restlessly, Gray swung his tall figure to the door, listened, and turned back. "No, I don't," he admitted. "But trim off those fat words. They choke me."

The Judge, imperturbable, knocked ash from his cigar. "All right, here's the meat of it. The Sierra Verde range is the key to the whole Upper Pecos. It's the heart of the high range. Some fair-sized outfits. Mostly old-timers. The rest follow their lead, more or less. The Sierra Verde Pool has nothing to do with the cattle and range. It's men and money."

He flicked the letter. "This came to me from a man I'm in touch with up there. He reports that those scalawags have not only banded together, they've also chipped in money to hire a bunch of gunhands. It's serious. It could spread like fire in a wind if it's not stamped out. Yet I can't afford an open fight against them, as you well know, Gray. That's the problem."

Gray sat down, his interest caught in spite of himself. "Sounds like they've got a good leader," he remarked. "A strong guiding hand. Who is he?"

"His name's Wallace — Russell Wallace. He owns the Twin Peaks brand. He seems to be the one man all the rest are willing to follow at any time without argument. Pooling their money is his idea, and he holds the war chest. Or so my man believes."

"The problem boils down to this Wallace, then. If you could get to him . . ."

"Glad you're using your head again." More nearly affable than Gray had ever before seen him, the Judge offered him a cigar. "Yes, I've tried that. The name of the man who sent me this report is Froke. He heads a small gang of stock thieves operating from up near the Sangres. I promised him ten thousand dollars if he'd get hold of Wallace and bring him to me."

"Dead?"

"No, alive, for a talk. A bullet won't solve this. The thing's too big, too well known. The solution is to bring in Wallace alive, then have him send word back to his Sierra Verde followers that he has seen the light and is convinced that progress is inevitable. If their war chest is captured too, so much the better, eh?"

"That alone would cripple 'em," Gray agreed. He was weighing the problem impersonally. "Costs money to hire fighting hands, and they'd want the best they could get. And without this Wallace . . . I don't guess he'd be easy to convince, even if you can get him here."

"It can be done, if he's at all reasonable. Getting him here is the difficulty. For a year, Froke has been after him. What I receive from Froke is reports such as this." The Judge touched the letter. "Another failure! Stiffening resistance! Wallace is too sharp for Froke. Well?"

"Send in sharper men, I'd say."

"I've done that. They let me down. A couple of them made it over the mountains to Colorado, last I heard. Froke never found out where the others went. Or so he says. I don't trust him. He wants that bonus, and to keep the field clear for himself he may have betrayed them."

"Damn bad setup!" Gray observed. "You haven't softened it a bit!"

The Judge nodded. "A tough job, yes. But think of the rewards. The man who captures their war chest is entitled to keep it. And for Wallace, delivered here alive, he'll earn ten thousand dollars. How are you off for money?"

Gray bit hard into his cigar, scowling. "Me?"

"Why, yes. You, of course, Gray." The pale

45

eyes surveyed him tranquilly. "You know you're through here, don't you? I'm offering you the chance of your life. Earn this stake and go your way. Make a fresh start somewhere far from here."

"Ordinarily," Gray said, "for that kind of money I'd take a stab at capturing *you*, Judge! But this Sierra Verde job is —"

"I don't pretend to offer it out of sentiment. It's simply that I believe you're the best one for the job. It needs a madman ripe for anything, and God knows that's you!"

"I'm not sure I want it."

The Judge smiled. "But you'll damned well take it, Gray! With that stake in mind, and your knack of getting things done, you might pull it off. It's a very long chance, but still you might . . . you might!"

"It's the next thing to suicide."

"For you, staying here is suicide itself!"

Riding northward up the wide and interminable valley of the Pecos, Gray scanned the country about him constantly. He bent close attention to its possible pitfalls, none to its bleak beauty, and kept in mind that ten thousand dollars. The size of the Judge's standing bounty on Russell Wallace in itself indicated the dangerousness and difficulties of the job. No telling where and when the hazards would start cropping up.

The river ran like a gold-flecked blue ribbon, sparkling in the hot sun, flanked by margins of grass and cottonwoods with tattered bark, through burned-out piñon hills that resembled a giant's dried mud pies studded with warped cloves. Far to the west, the Capitans ridged purple peaks against the burnished, cloudless sky. Eastward lay the long plains, furred over by the brownish-yellow of sun-cured grama.

Ten thousand dollars. A pile of hard cash. As much as a man could reasonably need for whatever suited his fancy: a wild fling, or a fresh start soberly undertaken. A stake to think about on this lonely ride up the Pecos. Gray was used to being solitary, but he liked having something to occupy his mind, to keep it from slipping into the past.

"Bring in Wallace and the war chest both, and I'll add an extra bonus," the Judge had promised before Gray rode out of Blakeville. "I'll be generous. Especially if you get it done in time for me to break that standout crowd of scalawags before roundup's over."

"Want me to leave right away?"

"Sooner the better. You should be there in three days, unless you meet trouble on the way. Their town is Trail Fork. You've never been there, and they don't know you, but

47

step very light. They —"

"You giving me instructions how to go about it?"

"No, you don't need any that I could give you. Be on your way."

Beneath his pondering, Gray kept note of a horseman coming up the trail behind him. The man must have ridden out of Blakeville an hour or two after his own departure, but he didn't recognize the horse, a light buckskin, very distinctive whenever it showed up against the dark, stunted piñones. He was far in the rear, and had held to the same distance since Gray first sighted him.

Gray hipped around in his saddle. Squinting against the sun's brilliance, he scanned the far-off rider. He frowned, unable to detect anything familiar about him at that distance. It was possible that the man was hanging back to escape the dust raised by Gray's shuffling big sorrel. Or maybe he was a loner who didn't care for company. On the other hand, if he was a Blakeville man, it was somewhat odd that he should be traveling this route with apparently steady purpose. Where this route led, Blakeville men found no welcome.

Gray disliked having anyone dog along behind him, even beyond rifle rang in open country. He watched the buckskin and rider vanish down a dip of the trail and, in a mood of speculation mingled with some dour humor, he decided to make a test. He reined his sorrel horse off the trail, heeled it to a canter around the nearest low hill, and there drew in.

Cuffing back his hat, he thumbed sweat from his forehead. He slid his carbine up and down in its saddle scabbard, built a cigarette, and patiently waited. The rider of the buckskin would notice his line of tracks, no doubt of that. If he had the right kind of savvy, he would take the hint. That joker had better ride right on by, not staring too inquisitively, if he understood the correct rules of health.

But the joker didn't follow the rules. Gray was smoking his second cigarette when the muted crunch of hoofs in sand reached him. He pinched out the cigarette, rose in his stirrups, and scanned the trail.

The man on the buckskin came to where Gray's tracks bent off. He reined over, following them deliberately, and walked his horse around the hill. Gray, expressionless, gazed at red hair, yellow eyes, and a face the color of old saddle leather.

"Good afternoon, Mr. Gray!" said Bas Tomayo.

4
PECOS PILGRIMS

Keeping his thoughts to himself, Gray demanded curtly, "What the devil are you doing here?"

Smiling, Bas Tomayo returned his gaze, and then suddenly Gray perceived that the yellow eyes contained a look that had not been in them in Blakeville. This was a changed Tomayo, not at all humble. His smile was lightly laced with impudent mockery. He had shed a guise.

He took off his hat. It had a flat crown, wide brim, and chin strings. His fiery hair stuck up like a circus clown's outlandish wig. He smoothed it down with his palm, watching Gray intently.

"Funny little man, aren't I, Mr. Gray?"

His speech bore only the barest trace of accent, and that not typically Mexican but of some other foreign source, cultured, utterly unlike the broken English he had affected while in Blakeville. He uttered a liquid giggle bereft of mirth, his shallow smile deepening.

"A ludicrous example of miscegenetic mischance! Am I not, Mr. Gray?"

He wore different clothes now, one reason

why Gray had not recognized him at a distance. An air of elegance, close to dandyism, hung about him. His shirt was of heavy white silk. His riding boots had the rich grain of fine leather, and the Mexican spurs were silver. He wore his gun low in a cutout holster; there was also a businesslike bulge under his right armpit.

Making his extraordinary remarks about himself and his bizarre appearance, he maintained his bright regard on Gray.

Not having the faintest notion of what a "miscegenetic mischance" might mean, and doubting if it was worth worrying about at the moment, Gray demanded again, "What're you doing here?"

The bright, expectant glimmer faded in the yellow eyes. Bas Tomayo replaced his hat on his head and fingered the chin strings thoughtfully. It was as if Gray had in some way disappointed him. He stopped smiling. His mouth moved down at the corners.

"I'm trailing you," he answered blandly. "That should be obvious."

"It is. What's your reason?"

"Judge Blake's orders."

Gray scowled. "And what's *his* reason?"

"Isn't that a forbidden question, generally speaking? His Honor the Judge" — Tomayo pronounced the title solemnly, raising his hat in mock reverence — "is a man who, pursuing his large destiny, doesn't let his right hand know what his left is doing. In this case, however, his motive is clear. This will explain it." He extracted a note from his shirt pocket and, edging his horse forward, handed it to Gray.

The note read: *Tomayo knows the country up there. Use him.* It was signed by the Judge.

"I am here as your guide, back-watcher, and all-round little helper," Tomayo murmured. "You don't seem pleased to have me." His eyes took on that bright expectancy. "Why?"

"This was s'posed to be a one-man job," Gray said. "My job. Nothing against you, but I was set to go it alone."

"You'll find me useful."

"I don't question that."

This odd little joker, Gray concluded, had seen much of life, and was well acquainted with death. Probably a killer. A strain of chill viciousness lurked behind the insincere smile.

Tomayo coughed gently, retrieving the note from Gray's hand and tearing it into confetti. "His Honor chose me for my rather special qualifications. My orders are to help you stay alive, to carry out a task that is, ah, fraught with peril. We are forced to trust each other, aren't we, Mr. Gray?"

That placed it squarely on the line. *"Es verdad, señor,"* Gray said. He drew his brows down, staring back over the empty trail. "But I think you're here to see that I don't run out on the Judge without him knowing about it, damn him!"

"You speak Spanish?"

"I've lived in Mexico. Well, let's push on." Gray lifted his reins. "No, friend, don't drop behind me! Makes me uncomfortable, much as we trust each other. I don't need anybody to watch my back. We'll ride together."

Bas Tomayo inclined his head in polite assent. He glanced quizzically several times at Gray as they rode on up the trail. It was some time before he asked, "Why so solemn, Mr. Gray? Don't you ever laugh?"

The question, unexpected as it was, hardly penetrated into Gray's silent meditations. There had been a time when laughter came easily to him. "What's there to laugh about?" he responded absently.

"Not much," Tomayo conceded. "Yet I can laugh, and look what I am!" His laugh came thin and tinny. "A biological freak! A funny little hybrid —"

"Why so sorry for yourself, *señor?*" Gray

interrupted.

Angry resentment flashed in the yellow eyes. Then Bas Tomayo laughed again. "Do you know what I'm talking about?"

Gray shook his head briefly. "Frankly, I don't give a damn. Look, Tomayo —"

"I was born in the Yucatan. My father was Castilian, an *aristo,* one of the redheaded, blue-blooded Tomayos. My mother was Indian, a root-grubbing savage of the lowest class."

"O.K., so you're a Yucatano. I still don't give a damn. If we're going to get along together, you'll have to learn to shut up."

"I'll try," Tomayo promised. "I was told you were tough and a bit, ah, strange. Damned if you're not! We'll get along together, Mr. Gray."

"Drop the 'Mister,' huh?"

"Yes, Gray. It wasn't intended as complimentary."

"I didn't think it was."

They exchanged no further words until they made camp that night. Camp was a dry one, their canteens having to suffice, for the trail they now followed was the forsaken old Espejo, which angled away from the river. Few traveled it these days. They camped without a fire, too, although the air grew chilly after dark. A fire might be seen for miles. There had to be no forewarning of their coming from Blakeville.

Their first object was to get up into the Sierra Verde, the cattle country lying between the old Espejo Trail and the Estancia plains, without arousing notice. After that, Gray figured, it would be best to proceed openly, acting the part of cowpunchers riding the grub line from somewhere east of the Pecos, looking for roundup jobs. Innocent strangers. Well, anyhow, strangers. They couldn't pass for innocent, with their looks. Troubleshooters on the loose, they were, for hire to the first bidder.

Returning from staking out his buckskin horse, Tomayo remarked, "Fine bright moon, for Comanches and thieves. 'How oft hath yonder moon . . .' " He shivered, broke off that classic quotation, and muttered another: " 'Till this outworn earth be dead, as yon dead world the moon.' Hmm! Your somber mood is catching, Gray!"

"Here, have a cigar. Extra one the Judge gave me. Don't like 'em much, myself."

"Thank you. Do you actually prefer the chopped straw and dried cow dung that you call cigarette tobacco? It's a depraved taste. A mark of plebeian coarseness."

"Go to hell," Gray said companionably.

"I shall arrange to have trumpets and a

plush carpet ready for you there. No vintage wine or champagne — you wouldn't appreciate it."

"Put me down for whiskey and a beer chaser," Gray yawned. "G'night, friend."

There was no reply. Bas Tomayo shook out his saddle blanket and, lighting the gift cigar, lay smoking, arms folded behind his head. Gray was close to sleep when he heard the little Yucatano mutter, "Good night, friend."

On the last word Tomayo injected a lingering note of query, like a sneer — *"friend?"* — as if it were a false word that he distrusted, as if he had never heard that word used before.

The glowing end of the cigar was mashed viciously into the sand. Tomayo sat up, took a last look around, and got under his blanket. He grunted something that had the sound of an obscene curse and then breathed quietly, not stirring in the silence, glaring up at the remote round glob of moon.

5
BLAKEVILLE MEN BEWARE

In the town of Trail Fork, hub of the Sierra

Verde, it appeared that no improvements had been added for the past forty years, and at the sight of it, Gray guessed it would remain so for forty more.

Its weathered old buildings formed a loose cluster at the fork of two trails, one from the east, the other from the south. The trails meandered across country, splitting off here and there like the strands of a frayed rope. There was no stage line, only a local freighting outfit. Its isolation had stamped a hidebound conservatism upon the little cowtown. It shunned anything new, and would have no traffic with strangers. The signs were visible.

Gray had known its jealously self-contained like before. So had Bas Tomayo, evidently, for he murmured, "Here are the prize mossbacks! They'd damn the new moon for displacing the old one." Gray remembered then that Tomayo was acquainted with this Sierra Verde country. Tomayo disclaimed ever having visited Trail Fork before, but he knew its kind of people.

The keeper of the one general store would not give information to the pair of dusty strangers. He made no bones about it. He admitted to being a Sierra Verde man from way back, and judging by his leathery face and limping gait, he had been a cowman until too many rough horses stove him up, but beyond that meager admission, there was no budging him. The front of his store was without name or sign. Everybody knew where and what the store was and who owned it, so there wasn't much point in publishing such facts.

"Wallace?" he echoed. "Russell Wallace?" He raised a cogitative squint at the ceiling, his elbows spread on the counter. His voice boomed a lot louder than was necessary. "Twin Peaks, you said, or was it Pin Creeks? Or did you mean Tin —"

"You got it the first time," Gray said.

Some men idling in the store turned from fingering new bridles. The women filed out as though someone had used foul language, their shopping unfinished, silent for once under the stern glances of their taciturn lords and masters.

"Never heard of him or any brand like that'n round here!" declared the storekeeper. "Pin or tin, it don't strike my recollection."

It was Gray's doing, this inquiring openly for Russell Wallace and the directions to Twin Peaks. If Wallace was recruiting a fighting force, as reported, there was nothing unusual in a couple of riders wanting to get in touch with him. Gray had thought it

58

the wise course for him and Tomayo to establish themselves as prospective gunhands for the Sierra Verde Pool, seeing there was no other plausible reason for their presence.

Bas Tomayo wasn't sold on the idea, for some reason best known to himself. But he strung along, with insolent eyes and sardonic jibes that seemed purposely aimed at irritating Gray, who was getting about enough of him.

"What can I sell you?" the storekeeper barked. "Mister, you're wastin' my time!"

Gray slapped a dollar down on the counter. There was no sense in calling the man a liar to his face, though the temptation to do so was strong. It was unbelievable that anyone here didn't know Russell Wallace, head of the Sierra Verde Pool, and his Twin Peaks outfit.

"You can sell me" — Gray glanced along the shelves of merchandise and named the first thing that came to mind — "pins. A packet o' pins."

"Tin pins?" inquired the storekeeper, taking the dollar, and from Tomayo came a maliciously appreciative chuckle.

That was too much. "Stick 'em in your rump!" Gray growled and walked out, Tomayo after him.

It was month-end Saturday, and the town was fairly full of cowfolks. Soon, as the sun dipped down, the women and most of the family men would be pulling out, buckboards and spring wagons loaded with a month's staple supplies, homeward bound to the ranches. The unmarried men, staying over for their fling at bottle and cards, would straggle back at all hours and tomorrow fight their headaches. Come Monday, come work. Cow country.

The town supported only one saloon, big as a barn and bearing a sign out front that said it was the Union Bar. Not a common name this close to Texas. Trail Fork was evidently of Northern inclination. The Territory had swayed toward the Confederate cause in the Civil War, and among the factors that held it to the Union was its leavening of Northern settlers. Gray pushed into the Union Bar, not looking back to see if Tomayo was still with him and not much caring.

The saloon held a crowd, but it wasn't noisy. Unlike the pugnacious loafers of Blakeville, these were working cowmen who conversed in easy tones and savored their drinks leisurely with some semblance of discretion. They addressed one another familiarly, in the dry manner of old friends and neighbors. The Sierra Verde range had been settled a long time. Its people were closely knit in spite of distances, everybody knowing everybody else. It wouldn't have been possible for a couple of strangers to scout around anywhere in it unnoticed.

"Twin Peaks?" The bartender to whom Gray put his casual question didn't take the line the storekeeper had taken. "It's right where it's always been!" He had uncorked a bottle. He thumped the cork back and planted his hands flat on the bar, and Gray was aware of quietness spreading about him.

As in the general store, he had brought this on himself by trying a straightforward approach. Here was the same ready suspicion, unveiled hostility, probing eyes that let it be known they did not like what they saw. It was too late for him to try a different tack. The presence of Bas Tomayo, who had followed him in, served only to alienate the crowd still further.

Tomayo was more of a liability than an asset, and Gray inwardly cursed the Judge for sending him along. As a guide, he had not been very helpful so far, being one of those who seemingly couldn't give the simplest directions clearly, for when Gray asked him the location of Wallace's outfit, he was so confusingly vague that Gray gave it up as a bad job.

Arms folded, the Yucatano regarded the crowd, his expression exasperatingly superior, as if he were inspecting a colony of termites with considerable distaste. Men didn't like him at first glance, as he unmistakably knew. His touches of elegance in dress and manner, his effeminate features, sneering yellow eyes — everything about him, including his small size and the color of his smooth skin, was anathema to average men.

And he flung his obnoxious strangeness into their stony faces, flaunted it as if he relished their antipathy. In his company, coupled with him, any man laid himself open to criticism. Tomayo took off his hat, and somehow that act, ordinary in itself, caused Gray to flush.

The cowmen stared at that grotesque shock of incredibly red hair. By some trick in the way he whipped off his hat, Tomayo had made it to shoot up in all directions. Combing his fingers through it, he stared back at them.

"Why d'you want to know about Twin Peaks?" the bartender asked Gray bluntly. "Where you from?"

"East," Gray said. He and Tomayo had skirted wide around and entered Trail Fork by the east trail.

More men came into the Union Bar, most of whom had been in the general store when Gray inquired there. They exchanged solemn nods with the men present and halted inside the swing doors, gazing like all the rest at Gray and Tomayo.

Gray wished that he had taken the trouble to learn the lay of Twin Peaks before leaving Blakeville. He might then have thought twice before pulling this blunder. His neglect of forethought bothered him, made him wonder if he was growing too careless. Nor did he have any description of Russell Wallace. The man could be here in the Union Bar right now, among his friends and backers. The bartender would bear close watching.

The bartender opened his mouth to say something, then paused because Gray was looking straight at him. Sizing up the temper of the big stranger, the bartender passed the cue to his customers. "These fellers want the way to Twin Peaks!"

Nobody picked it up. The crowd went on inspecting the ill-matched pair. Giving them something to watch, Gray plucked the bottle from the bartender's hand and drew the cork. The bartender retreated without payment. Gray filled two shot glasses, handed one to Tomayo, and swung half around from the bar. Tomayo, a head taller than the bartop, raised his glass to Gray in an unspoken toast, and they drank together.

Finally a voice rasped, "Who are they?"

The owner of the voice stood with a group at the dice table, where they had been shaking for drinks. He was of middle age, heavy, red-faced, with bull eyes and a tilt to his head that bannered a flaring belligerence. He was plainly a man of standing whose attitude could set the example to others, for his loud demand started a slow surge of movement. His group quit the dice table to range up alongside him. The men at the bar slid away from Gray and Tomayo, leaving them room enough for a dance.

Those at the door closed ranks and stood pat. One of them called to the red-faced man, "And who sent 'em? Ask 'em that, Marley!"

"Ask me!" put in the bartender from a reasonably prudent position at the far end of the bar. "I can smell Blakeville bait!"

"That's not hard," a lanky rancher observed. He added with heavy humor, "After all, it's coming time the Judge sent us up another candidate!"

Gray and Tomayo placed their emptied glasses on the bar and didn't replenish them. It was not comfortable to drink there in front of the hostile crowd. It was a lonely spot to be in, listening to caustic comments aimed obliquely at them.

"We wouldn't want to feel the Judge was neglectin' us!"

"Y'know, some dark an' dreary day he'll get damn-right real annoyed —"

"And send the Lobo? That'll be a big day!"

"Let's look forward to it. Hell, his second best ain't hardly give us a good workout! Who's scared o' the Lobo?"

"Don't name no names. Yours might crop up! Lobo Gray's a killer. I'm satisfied to meet the second best, an' so're you!"

Gray tightened up. Hearing his name spoken, in that way and in those terms, shot a tingle through him. He had not realized that his reputation had grown so tall, so sinisterly repellent, afield from Blakeville and the Judge's bailiwick.

The talk took a turn away from obliqueness and toward directness.

"What d'you reckon the Mex midget's here for?"

These Sierra Verde cowfolks were not fighters by trade, but they were proddy. They stuck together, despite their squabbling. They had so far defied the Judge and settled the hash of the Judge's scouts. Success bred confidence.

"The fancy little Mex? Well, my outfit could sure use a roundup cook, but I doubt he's fittin'. I can't stomach them chili beans."

That made it too direct. They were trespassing outside the limits of impersonal comment. Gray, elbows hooked onto the edge of the bar behind him, ran a slowly regarding stare over the speakers. He mentally scored up a mark to Tomayo's credit for holding himself in against insult, and he said to him, "These folks don't have good manners."

Tomayo appeared not to hear him and began to edge off, evincing nervousness as the remarks verged into denunciations.

"How're things down in Blakeville?"

"How's the Judge?"

Marley, the red-faced man, flapped a beefy paw. "Pipe down everybody, I'll do the talking!" he announced. His type was not rare — a man who mistook loudness for toughness and got away with it by virtue of his age and local standing. At a guess, Gray took him to be Russell Wallace's number-one backer. As such, in Wallace's absence Marley was exerting himself to take command of the situation.

Something of a gunfighter as well, this

Marley. Knew the principles, anyway, judging from the hang of his holster. Points and circumstances lodged in Gray's mind while his finger muscles tensed. It was like a thing apart from himself, that slight, preparatory tensing. Always at this point, his mind calmed and he became as observant of his own actions as a critical spectator.

Marley sent a look to the men blocking the swing doors. Gray intercepted it and read its message. He was already tried and convicted. These men lost no time. By his own reaction, he had given them their cue: a guiltless stranger would have argued and protested at the first spoken suspicion that he was an enemy gunman from Blakeville. He had not done so, and that was enough for them.

Still, Marley had proposed to do the talking, and though clearly little remained to be talked over, he had to go on and say something. "A while ago, I asked a question and didn't get no answer!" he bellowed. "In case somebody's deaf, I'll repeat it! Who? . . ."

"*Señor!*" piped up Bas Tomayo urgently. "I no friend thees *hombre!*" He pointed a shaking finger at Gray and sidled farther away from him. "No friend! We jus' meet on trail, *esta día.* We ride along. I dunno heem! *Sabe, señor?*"

After a moment of solemn surprise, a snicker broke out. "He sure didn't get no sand with that red hair!" a young puncher commented. "Never saw a scareder Mex!"

"Heem no friend me! *Es verdad — por Dios, es verdad!*" Tomayo's voice thinned to a falsetto squeak. "*Señores,* I work, get *dinero,* now I go home *Mejico.* I good *hombre,* no bad!"

"*Hombre* means a man," said the young puncher, "an' that's the part I sure doubt! The rest sounds about right, don't it? I'll say this much for the Judge — he don't hire that kind o' critter!"

Marley assented with a profoundly sagacious nod. "You can go," he told Tomayo. "Beat it! Get on your horse and go home *Mejico.* Be careful next time who you fall in with on the road — it can get you in trouble!"

"*Gracias, señores — mil gracias!*"

Bobbing his head to everybody, Tomayo let out gasps of thankfulness. The men inside the swing doors parted to let him through, somewhat hurriedly and widely, as though they wanted to avoid any accidental contact with him. Donning a pathetic semblance of his former jauntiness, Tomayo minced across the floor, lisping persistently, "*Mil gracias . . . mil gracias . . .*"

Gray took his gaze off the little deserter, feeling nothing but a contemptuous compassion for him, but that feeling passed when he looked at the faces of the crowd. Whatever measure of tolerance and forbearance the Sierra Verde cowmen may have possessed, they had spent it in letting Tomayo go. Whatever suspension of judgment may have briefly existed, there was none now for him, the big fellow standing on his own, alone as for years he had been essentially alone — himself, Lobo Gray.

"All right," he said to them. "Let's have it!"

6
HOMBRE MEANS A MAN

In the stillness resulting from Gray's terse invitation, the atmosphere of the Union Bar had the pregnant solemnity of a courtroom gripped by the moment between the tapping gavel and the pronouncement of sentence. The undercurrent of violence showed only in the eyes of the men, who were watching Gray, paying concentrated heed to his slightest move.

They were set for Marley's prompting signal, waiting for it because Marley had taken charge and because not one of them measured up to the title of gunman. A prickly bunch of cowmen, rabidly independent and with the fighting edge, but unskilled in the deadly craft of the fast draw. Hard work gnarled the fingers that, for gun speed, needed to be as flexible and sensitive as those of a cardsharp.

Pressure was the last bet left, a thousand-to-one chance of bluffing them out of their resolve to take concerted action. Gray said directly to Marley, "How much time d'you think you've got?"

"Why, I —" Marley began, taken aback, and shut his teeth with a click. He jerked his right hand. The men about him copied his gesture readily. The bartender ducked beneath the bar and came up again immediately.

Gray stroked his guns out. The right-hand one, chopping aside, blared once before it straightened out level with its mate to cover Marley and the crowd. The bartender, too eager for his own good, dropped a sawed-off shotgun and clutched a smashed hand to his chest.

Marley and the crowd, momentarily frozen in attitudes of unfinished action, glared at Gray, and he glared back. He had them stopped only briefly. They were far too many for any one man to hold in check for long. Yet neither could he get out of the Union Bar without showing his back to at least some of them.

"Damn, but they're slow!" drawled Bas Tomayo from the swing doors. Heads swiveled in his direction, and there was a shocked widening of eyes.

His frightened simper was gone. In its place was the faint, false smile that he had worn when he caught up with Gray on the trail and spoke to him, and his speech carried the same exaggerated ring of culture. He held a gun in each hand, one from his holster, the other plucked from under his silk shirt.

His yellow eyes glittered with a wicked maliciousness that made the cowmen nearest the swing doors draw away, as they had drawn away from him before, though now for a different reason. He seemed suddenly to have grown to twice his former size. The effeminate little craven of a minute ago was transformed into a menacing killer, nerveless, chillingly malignant.

"*Hombre* means a man!" he intoned softly. Smiling, he turned his nightmarish eyes upon the young cowpuncher who had said it and had appended a slur to it. "It does indeed!"

His gaze exuded a deadly evil, an unforgiving hatred for them all. They had placed upon him the exigency of playing the part of a despised and cowardly freak before them, at bitter cost to his self-esteem. They had snickered at him as something less than a man, something far inferior to them.

"To stamp on a man's ego is dangerous!" he said to the young cowpuncher. "To rob a man of his personal psyche, even for a moment — especially when I am the man — is madness! I single you out for illustration. Down on your knees, lout!"

Scarcely understanding Tomayo's words, but understanding the command to kneel and objecting to it, the young cowpuncher dug desperately for his gun. Tomayo, still smiling, shot him in the stomach. The cowpuncher floundered to the floor, moaning, and Tomayo's glittering eyes searched for the next victim.

Gray stepped through the spellbound crowd, saying, "The joke's on you, fools!"

The joke was on him, too. Seldom had he seen a jackpot tipped over so neatly and unexpectedly — and without much help from him, although maneuvered on his behalf. Tomayo had succeeded in completely fooling him along with the crowd and had gained the upper hand by a simple but perfectly performed act of unabashed treachery. The thought recurred to Gray that perhaps he was losing his perceptive edge, that perhaps he was slipping. That fatal time was bound to come if a man stayed with the game.

Tomayo, dangling his guns, was inquiring silkily, "Why the silence? Has a sudden epidemic of lockjaw struck this fair community?" He addressed Marley. "Such a short time ago you were the spokesman, loud and positive . . ."

Marley remained like an image, legs spread apart, head at a pugnacious tilt. The Sierra Verde cowmen stared stonily at Tomayo's guns, at Gray's guns. They let the weighted seconds drag by, without completing the holsterbound strokes of their taut hands. Not from lack of bull courage, obviously, but from common-sense caution, Marley took the little Yucatano's searing sarcasm:

". . . And now you have nothing to say! This is surely an unusual access of modesty on your part!" Wagging his scarlet-crowned head, Tomayo languidly lined a gun at Marley's paunch. "I can cure you of it, with pleasure!"

He had to be prevented from indulging himself in an orgy of vengeful slaughter.

Gray, taking a slow step toward him, aiming to sidetrack him, said to him quietly, "Let's mosey the hell out of here, Don Basilio!"

It fetched him a sharp look from Tomayo and a crisp rejoinder. "*Señor,* I would not have thought this an occasion for pseudo-formality!"

"Not pseudo," Gray said. The little killer had a chip on his shoulder. Perhaps he could be kidded out of it. "A slip of the tongue. I meant to say Don Tomato . . ." And he readied himself for possible fireworks, knowing it was a tossup.

Tomayo chuckled, his face clearing. "A bad joke is worse than none, but that's so bad it's funny! Don Tomato! I think we need a breath of air. Shall we seek, ah — ?"

"A cheerier climate?"

"A refreshing atmosphere, I was about to say. A pure and cleansing wind, to rid you of the odor of that joke."

"Yeah. You stink a bit, too."

They backed together to the swing doors, two gunfighters at bay seeking the breeze, making dryly insulting remarks to each other to sustain their arrogant comradeship. They both knew it was touch-and-go whether or not they got alive out of the Union Bar and Trail Fork.

In a dead hush, the younger cowmen in

74

the barroom breathed deeply, their nostrils pinching in and swelling, their mouth muscles bunched. They wanted to fight. Some of the older men darted half-expectant glances toward Marley, spokesman, acting leader.

By those glances, it was manifest that Russell Wallace was nowhere within call. Marley was standing in for the kingpin of Sierra Verde, but only within narrow limits did he hold any actual power. What the men were looking for from him was not a commanding signal, but a hotheaded play that would open up the opportunity for them to swing into action.

Marley did nothing of the kind. He stood transfixed, his large face congested with rage, his eyes burningly watchful.

Most of this crowd must have ridden in from the roundup camps for the Saturday fling in Trail Fork. It was the time in this high country for the summer work to be heading along at full drive. Gray doubted if any of the Twin Peaks riders were present here. Somehow, by his name and leading personality, Russell Wallace sounded like the dour kind of Scotsman who kept his crew sweating eighteen hours a day, seven days a week, and wouldn't abide any form of high jinks. If he wasn't out bossing the work tonight, he'd most likely be home poring through tally books and ledgers.

Gray decided that the best bet now was to head straight for the Twin Peaks outfit, if Tomayo really knew its location. It would have to be done fast, before the alarm spread that a pair of gunslinging strangers were on the loose. He and Bas Tomayo needed a load of luck.

The luck arrived right then, all of it bad.

It began with a floorboard. Countless hard-heeled boots for many years had clumped in and out of the Union Bar, and under the long punishment one of the floorboards at the entrance had become loosened and warped. It rocked when trod on. In all likelihood the regular customers had gained a semiconscious awareness of it and stepped over it without giving it a thought. Tomayo had no knowledge of it, and he was stepping backward.

His right boot came down on the faulty floorboard. The board rocked. So did Tomayo. And in recovering his balance he hung his left spur in the tipped-up edge.

Don Basilio Tomayo teetered. He vanished from Gray's side. He took a backward header, knocked the swing doors wide open, and tumbled down three wooden steps to the boardwalk outside.

"What the hell's he up to now?" Gray muttered, thinking it another of the Yucatano's unexpected tricks, although he couldn't see much purpose in it.

He halted his own back-stepping retreat, keeping the barroom covered, his forearms clamped to his ribs, guns poking. The swing doors flapped smartly back and inward on their two-way hinges, hit both of his elbows a hard crack, and the jolt set off the hair triggers of his cocked guns. The bullets split a shelf of the backbar and brought a mirror down in slivers.

The barroom crowd, jumping to the conclusion that he had gone trigger-mad, and lacking any further incentive to stand still, came stampeding at him in a wild rush. Gray dived out, missing the steps and colliding into Tomayo on the boardwalk.

Bounding to his feet and swearing in a mixture of languages, Tomayo chopped two shots and punched a hole dead in the center of each swaying door of the Union Bar. His face was savage. He waved a smoking gun. "Our horses!" he snarled, and one look told Gray what he meant.

Their two horses were missing from the hitchrack of the general store where they had tied up. Not only that, but there wasn't a horse left in sight. Somebody had gathered them and led them off, against the off-chance that the two inquiring strangers managed to stage a break. Trail Fork was out to stop them from proceeding any further and didn't mind taking some trouble to make it a certainty.

A voice rapped from a doorway, "Throw down your guns, you two! This is the sheriff!" Without pause or further notice, a rifle cut loose. That sheriff craved quick service. He got it.

Gray dropped twistingly down on one knee, threw up a gun, and fired. He saw the sheriff heave into sight and reel back into his doorway. The saloon crowd remained inside for the time being, steadied by the bullet holes in the door, hoping for the sheriff to get in his lick with the rifle. Gray made a lurching run into the alley across from the Union Bar. The sheriff got off another hasty shot at him, shouting, "Dammit, fellers, come out here an' give me a hand!"

Already in the alley ahead of him, Tomayo was shooting at the saloon, holding the crowd to cover. The little man's savage rage had passed as swiftly as it had come. A dispassionate calmness smoothed his tawny face. "Are you hit?" he asked Gray.

"Leg. That damn sheriff's rifle!"

"Makes it awkward," Tomayo commented lightly.

"Makes *me* awkward!" Gray said.

The sun sank behind the western hills. In the first tinge of dusk, subdued sounds issued from behind blank windows along the empty street. The town was quietly gathering itself together for an explosive effort.

"I noticed a corral as we came in," Gray said. "Back of the freight house. Bunch of mules penned there. Maybe you saw them, did you?"

Tomayo nodded, holding his guns trained on the Union Bar. "Speaking of jackasses," he murmured, "we certainly messed up this job!"

"It's a bust," Gray agreed. "Those jiggers will be all round us any minute now, and then it'll be over. You know it. So you better try for that corral and pick yourself a mule that can run."

Tomayo took his gaze off the saloon doors and scanned Gray's scarred and beard-stubbled face. "We might both try," he suggested, but his voice lacked conviction.

Gray's short laugh was harshly derisive. "Me ride a mule bareback with this leg? Get out o' here while you can and don't argue the deal!"

Tomayo smiled. A smoky veil darkened

79

his eyes. He leaned over as if to nudge Gray or to offer him a helping arm, then drew back without touching him. His smile tuned false, and the yellow eyes mirrored once more the insolent mockery. "Shall I convey your regards to His Honor?" he inquired.

Flat and abrupt, a gun spat from the Union Bar. Before it could set off a volley and a rush, Gray fired twice. A window's broken fragments tinkled, and a man's yell quavered like the call of an owl in the early evening. Gray then found that he was alone, for Tomayo had taken him at his word and gone running through the alley.

He didn't hold it against Tomayo. The little guy had backed him up pretty well in the Union Bar jackpot, but that didn't mean he could be expected to pass up a last chance at a getaway. Tomayo claimed no place among the old stock of gunfighters, those quiet-spoken men whose pride insisted that they give the other fellow an even break and whose code demanded that they stick with a wounded partner to the finish. That kind didn't belong on the Judge's payroll, anyway.

With the thought of the Judge, Gray cursed him. It came to him in a wave of repugnance that he was about to die in a dirty alley, shooting it out with men he didn't know and who certainly didn't know him, in a two-bit cowtown he'd never seen before. Just another Blakeville badman who went out on a job for the Judge and never got back.

"Me?" he growled. "Hell, no!"

He slammed three more bullets into the Union Bar, caving in the last of the front windows, and dragged himself down the alley. The sheriff's bullet had got him above the knee. His leg was numb, with only a tingle of pain as yet, and he felt the blood trickling down into his boot.

Tomayo had run left from the end of the alley, to work around to the mule corral, and there was no sign or sound of him now. Gray crawled to the right, toward the livery barn across from the general store. If he could slip in the back and get at the liveryman, hold a gun on him, make him saddle a horse . . .

He might manage to stay in a saddle long enough to break clear of this town and find some place where he could hole up — if he roped himself on, if the horse wasn't a buck-ee, and if the mob didn't hunt him down while he was still afoot. He knew he was leaving a trail of blood behind him that any fool could follow.

7
RENEGADE RODEO

Gray reached the rear of the livery by scraping through the pole fence into the yard. The yard was empty. The tall back doors of the barn were closed. They sagged on their hinges and met unevenly, and through the crack he could see that the bar was up on the inside. The liveryman had shut up shop and cautiously barred himself in until the town's disturbance was settled. Nobody, Gray mused bleakly, was overlooking any bets.

He was about to insert a gun barrel into the crack and try prying up the bar when he caught the sounds of a stamping hoof, a snort, and the faint creak of leather. The sounds came from close by. He moved on past the livery doors. He peered around the corner of the barn and checked a grunt of relief.

In the lane leading from the street back to the livery yard stood a buckboard and harnessed team that evidently had been backed in hastily off the street for safety. The two horses, good bays, had their heads bent in his direction, sniffing uneasily, ears cocked, aware of his presence before he appeared at the corner.

The smell of his blood made them nervous. His crawling advance scandalized them. The near horse crowded over against its mate. Gray couldn't give them a friendly cussing to lull their mistrust. The liveryman would hear him and raise the alarm.

The horses sidled off toward the street, conferring together in agitated snorts, wanting nothing to do with any blood-smelly hobgoblin who didn't walk upright and swear out loud. A noisy racket broke out in the street and switched their aroused fright in that direction. They paused to consider. Gray rose, hopped forward on his good leg, and floundered into the buckboard. He snatched up the lines, and the team stood, shivering but passive, recognizing the authority of human hands.

The racket in the street swelled louder, concentrated somewhere down past the Union Bar. Men were running, shouting. Some shots blared, and hoofs pounded hollowly on a boardwalk like drumbeats. It could have been an impromptu Saturday night rodeo — somebody having trouble with his mount, and everybody pulling for the horse. Gray coaxed the buckboard team forward and took a look. He had to get out by way of the street no matter what was going on. The lane was too narrow to turn in, not much wider than the buckboard, and it ended back in the livery yard at that.

It wasn't a fractious jughead that was raising the riot. It was a big Missouri mule, contrary by nature and with no saddle or sense to handicap him. Bas Tomayo was doing the riding, clinging on like a monkey and bouncing at every bump. He couldn't afford to let go, and there was always a wild chance at each twist that his long-eared steed might take a fit to leave town with him. He had picked himself a mule that could run, but whatever had since transpired between them was obviously all the mule's enterprise. The crowd complicated his dilemma, surging about, yelling, trying to box in the scampering mule and at the same time stay clear of its formidable hoofs.

A determined cowpuncher ran out at it, twirling a rope. The mule, knowing what that hated thing was, skidded half a turn in a boil of dust and flashed its hindhoofs at his face. The cowpuncher dodged them by a hair but got tangled in his loop and went down. Exasperated, he sat up, dragged out his gun, and blazed impartially at the animal and its jockey.

The mule took two jumps that landed it on the boardwalk near the Union Bar.

Startled at the loud booming under its own feet, it leaped off, threw a high roller, and came down stiff-legged.

Bas Tomayo's bobbing head snapped so low he kissed the brute's neck. But still he hung on somehow.

Thoroughly mad, the big mule uncorked a series of weaving bucks, shaking itself like a wet dog. It was a rapid display of acrobatics in which the object seemed to be to bite its own tail. Nobody could stay on the back of an ornery mule without its consent, and not always then. Tomayo had picked the wrong mule; or perhaps there weren't any right ones. It wound up the business by swapping ends faster than an inquisitive cat quitting an occupied kennel and won the trick.

Tossed wide, Bas Tomayo struck the Union Bar hitchrack and bounced off. He crouched on all fours in the dirt, his nose running blood, a cornered animal for the mob to blast to rags. The mule scooted back and forth, seeking an opening of escape in the closing circle of men.

Gray slapped the lines down on the team and let out an ear-splitting squawl. The team took off at a lunge, snapping his head back. As the buckboard shot out of the lane into the street both bays tried to swing away from the roaring commotion. He hauled their heads around, lashing them. It was a fast and cramped turn. The buckboard yawed over precariously on two wheels, the others spinning free. Banging into a porch post of the general store helped to right it, at the cost of the post, and Gray sent the team head on at the crowd.

Barely holding his balance on the seat while whacking the horses, he got only a rapid impression of faces whirling aside, a confused jumble of bodies, arms and legs flying, and thuds against the buckboard. The team burst through into the shrinking space before the Union Bar where the big Missouri mule cavorted and little Tomayo crouched.

"Up an' jump *amigo!*"

Whether or not Tomayo heard Gray's hail above the uproar, he didn't need the advice. It was that or be trampled by the charging bays. He upped and jumped in one nimble motion. There wasn't much room for him between the Union Bar hitchrack and the hurtling buckboard.

Rocking past, Gray took a hurried look back and could see nothing of Tomayo in the kicked-up dust. He guessed that the little man must have missed his jump and got left behind, if he wasn't hanging to the rear axle and dragging. He couldn't stop to find out. He charged on at the other half of the crowd, the mule seesawing ahead, thinking it was being pursued.

Breaking through this bunch was a livelier proposition. The others, their backs toward him when he drove at them, had been caught by surprise and followed their prompt impulse to scramble out of the path of what they supposed was a runaway team. This bunch, though, had a brief moment to see what was in the doing and who was coming at them, and they didn't propose to scatter.

Stopping a panicked pair of strong young horses wasn't any casual pastime, however, for men on foot in high-heeled boots — particularly with the horses following hard after a berserk mule and the buckboard driver laying about him furiously with the whip. Again came the mad turmoil of faces and bodies, but this time with hands clawing at the team.

The mule's progress loosened a hole in the crowd. The brute plunged on through, frantic, and so did the team close after it. One man clung stubbornly to the near horse, grabbing at the lines. Gray reached far over and clubbed the man, using the butt end of the whip. The man dropped off, rolling over and over on the ground. The raging cowmen behind hammered a flurry of shots after the careening buckboard.

An explosion of pain blinded Gray. He rode stiffly upright in the jouncing seat, shuddering uncontrollably, every muscle of his body taut, glaring into a dazzling white sheet of nothingness. Words formed in his mouth. He thought that he spoke them aloud, but his lips were clamped shut.

Goddam him to hell!

His curse was not aimed at the shooter whose bullet had found him, whoever he was. It was aimed at Judge Blake. In that instant, the blinding pain brought with it a stark clarity of mind which, like a lucid streak in the midst of delirium, brought forth a rational question: Had the Judge deliberately sent him here to his death?

There had been other henchmen who had grown moody and rebellious . . . men who had outlived their span of willing usefulness to the Judge. They were gunfighters, some of the old stock, who were unable to conceal a restless contempt for the Judge after learning too much about him. They were gone, killed in unexplained brawls and Blakeville flare-ups, or sent out on lone missions that turned out to be one-way trails.

And now he, Lobo Gray, the ramrod . . .

The white flare clouded, darkened swiftly to blackness that drowned thought. He was falling a great distance. He was falling alone, yet in his ear was Bas Tomayo's voice saying, "Stay with the rig, you big ox!"

Gray rose painfully back to the surface of consciousness, feeling that he was being forced up through layers of barbed wire and cactus while somebody thumped him regularly on the head with a sandbag. It was the intense pain that nagged him out of a dreaming reverie in which, on a long shot from his father's old percussion rifle, he had brought down a hawk. His father, in one of the rare sober periods since his mother's death, bawled him out for it. The hawk, which had flown like a winged spear in the sky, lay broken and ungainly from its plunge earthward.

"Never did you any harm, did it?" demanded his father. He had read a good deal in the happier days, and looking down at the dead hawk, he had said in the grave, troubled way that he had when he wasn't drinking, "God creates the living. He created this wild bird and gave it freedom. Gave it the power to live in its own fashion. Gave it the right to love . . ."

It was a lecture, winding up with a rebuke.

"And along comes you, a fool boy with a

89

gun" — his father looked away, bloodshot eyes hopeless, drowned in memory of the loved wife lost — "and slits the thin-spun thread of life!" he finished in a whisper.

The boy looked away, too, but only to hide his young intolerance. His father was getting queer in the head. Wouldn't kill anything, not even the thieving chipmunks that, grown bold in their immunity, scuttled and chattered under the floors of the house and raided the kitchen in broad daylight. He refused to carry a gun against the cattle thieves who robbed him poor. Yet it was said that the old man had been "considerable of a curly wolf, in his time."

That night, his father staggered in drunk and slapped him clear across the kitchen. "Too cussed handy wi' guns!" he shouted. "I ever catch you again — !"

Light penetrated Gray's eyelids. His will sluggishly fought the impulse to open his eyes. He wanted to go back to the ranch on the Nueces and tell his father that he understood him now, at least partly. But the reverie had dissipated in the wakening throb of pain, and he remembered with a dull regret that his father was long dead. He was not a boy anymore, not by a far cry. He was Lobo Gray, top gun of Blakeville.

Memory raced on, disclosing Trail Fork,

the Union Bar, the hostile Sierra Verde cow-men. The fight. The getaway. And there, against a wall of blinding white, memory faltered and came to a stop. Nothing existed for him beyond that.

Shocked to full pitch, consciousness swept away the cloudy lassitude and freed his mind to leaping speculation. A bullet had struck him in the head — yes, as he had raced out of Trail Fork in the stolen buck-board. What had happened to him after that? Where was he now?

He tested his wounded leg by flexing the tendons. The leg was bandaged above the knee. It hurt. Cautiously, he slid a hand up to his head. It was bandaged, too, and it throbbed sickeningly.

"Doctor!" exclaimed a low, clear voice, the voice of a woman. "I think he's —"

"Coming to? Good!" said a second voice that sounded crisply professional, yet famil-iar. "Tell me, do you have anything in the way of stimulants in the house?"

"Some whiskey?"

"Perhaps a small medicinal measure for my friend . . ."

"I'll go get it, Doctor."

"Thank you."

A door closed softly.

Gray opened his eyes. He was lying on a

bed in a lighted room. The bed sheets were fresh, and the room was furnished plainly but comfortably . . . a man's bedroom. Bas Tomayo's smooth brown face smiled down at him, the yellow eyes as bright as burnished brass. Gray had a string of questions to ask, and he began pouring them out.

"What's this place? Who's that woman? How — ?"

"Quiet!" Tomayo interrupted him. "I'll do the talking. We haven't much time. It shouldn't take her long to fetch the whiskey. I only asked for it to get her out before you could start blurting."

He darted to the closed door, put an ear to it, and returned to the bed.

"Now listen to this and try to keep it in your head!" he said rapidly. "I've changed our identities. You heard her call me 'Doctor'?"

"Doctor of what? Mules?"

"It so happens that I am not without a certain amount of medical background," Tomayo stated blandly. "For reasons we need not go into, I once posed as a surgeon in the Turkish Army, using forged papers. You see before you Dr. Euclides Maroon, a slightly eccentric foreign gentleman of private means, touring this barbarous land for his health, which suffered from overwork. Roughing it in the great outdoors. Going native, as it were, temporarily — which explains my garb and guns. Oh, I can carry it off all right!"

"You're the damnedest faker!"

"Two of us! You're Captain Walter Steel, my hired guide and companion, teaching me the curious customs of the country."

"Captain? I was only a corporal in —"

"I guessed you'd been some sort of military man for a while," Tomayo commented. "Our story is that we ran into a very unfortunate misunderstanding at Trail Fork. The strangest thing. They robbed us of our horses, then attacked us! For no reason whatever, unless it was a case of mistaken identity. We, the innocent victims, barely escaped with our lives!"

"I could cry for us," Gray grunted. "Say, the last I saw of you there, you'd missed the jump and gone under."

Tomayo shook his head. "No, I caught hold of the back of the buckboard. Climbed on just in time to keep you from falling off. Judas, how we smashed through that pack! You, the horses, the mule, and me — an effective combination. I must remember the technique. Still, I wouldn't mount a mule like that one again to skip hell. I'm sore all over."

He tenderly stroked his nose, which was swollen. "They got their horses and chased after us. For a while it was very awkward, driving the team and holding onto you as well. I was sorely tempted to let go of you."

"How come you didn't?" Gray asked him. "I didn't see you hold back from getting out of the alley when I told you to."

"That was different," Tomayo said evasively. "At any rate, I drove off the trail and hid in the brush. They tore past, terribly fierce, and for all I know they're still scouring south for us. Then I drove wide around cross-country and headed north. By the way, did you chance to notice the brand on those bays?"

"I was too busy. What was it?"

"Twin Peaks brand, interestingly enough. It seems that neighbor Marley borrowed them for his trip to town. He went in to pick up a new wheel for his own buckboard."

"How d'you know that?"

"I was told it when I dutifully delivered the team and rig home. Frankly, it's the first time I ever actually set foot on the place, but I feel we're going to like it."

Gray heaved a breath. "*What?* You mean — ?"

Bas Tomayo nodded airily. "Quite so, Gray

— Captain Steel, I mean! This is the Twin Peaks outfit. We are guests, uninvited, of course, but apparently not unwelcome, in the home of Russell Wallace!"

He raised a warning finger, listening, his head cocked. "She's coming back with the whiskey. Prepare yourself for another surprise, *mí capitán!* You'll get one, if you're half the man I think you are!"

8
RASCALS IN PARADISE

His first look at the woman who entered the room snatched Gray's thoughts up short. He stared, and his breath caught in his throat. Then an ache that was like a gnawing wrench of hunger clutched him inside. He bit back a strangled grunt.

There had been a few women who had affected him instantly, but none as strongly as this, and he had come to harden himself to the miragelike dissolving of that effect in the same moment. In the kind of life he had led for years, women did not occupy high pedestals. They took their social standing according to the flame of their attraction, and toward them men were not required to observe the strictest laws of decorum. The other kind, the kind Gray very rarely met, always caused him to become more stiffly reticent than usual. *They* were untouchable, and for that reason he guarded himself against having any feeling about them.

This woman was of that kind: *Do Not Touch! Do Not Stare Too Long!* In this Southwest country, the rules were inflexible.

But Gray's guard lay shattered. He could not take his eyes off her.

She had a wealth of raven hair, and her eyes were deep emerald. Feminine eyes. Her skin had a satin fineness, her lips were full, and she was young. She possessed something else besides visible beauty, something more, a warm quality not easy to define; it touched the senses. It touched and withdrew into the decorous envelope. It belonged in the realm of womanhood where, behind ramparts, passion and compassion waited with a boundless capacity to love the invader.

Her inquiring gaze went directly to the bed as soon as she entered and met Gray's fixed stare. She did not to avoid it, but held it steadily for a few seconds, after which her eyes lingered briefly on his face, his heavy stubble of beard, his many scars. Then, apparently having scrutinized him as much as she cared to, she looked away.

Tomayo, on his best behavior, relieved her of the tray she was carrying and set it down. "Our patient is doing rather well." He bowed to her, gesturing with a graceful wave of his hand toward Gray. "Miss Wallace, allow me to present Captain Steel." From his manner, he might have been at a royal court, presenting a deserving commoner to a princess. But, unseen by her, his eyes glimmered with quizzical amusement.

Her gaze met Gray's once more. Tomayo's impeccable formality imposed a restraint upon them both. They murmured an exchange of empty greetings. Gray didn't know what he said. He went on looking at her. And, as before, she made no pretense of being unaware of his persistently straight regard. It could not be ignored, and now a faint flush crept into her cheeks.

Tomayo, missing nothing, broke the awkward moment by saying to her, "I have been telling Captain Steel about my difficulties after I saved him from those ruffians in Trail Fork. That was a dastardly attack, Miss Wallace! An unprovoked outrage! The proper authorities at your nation's capital shall hear of it, mark my words! Why, the Captain would have been murdered had it not been for me!" He coughed modestly. "Fortunately, I was able to secure a mule and dash to his rescue."

"A mule?" She regarded him with some surprise. He was so small, so bizarre in appearance and manner, that it was difficult to visualize him as the heroic rescuer. An eccentric foreign gentleman of exquisite courtesy — yes, he fitted that role, but scarcely the part of a man of violence. "But it was a buckboard you brought him here in, Doctor. Our buckboard."

The kindly and indulgent smile that Tomayo bent upon her conveyed the intimation that she, as a member of the fair and sheltered sex, would naturally pick at that trifling detail. "The Captain doesn't know very much about how to ride a mule, you see," he murmured in confidential explanation and changed the subject.

"Ah, what a blessed angel of mercy you are to us in our sore distress!" he orated, expending another of his courtly bows upon her. "We were beset by perils, strangers in a hostile land, and you took us in!"

"Well, when you came in driving our buckboard —"

"In my country, a dying man will spend his last breath to restore lost property to its owner!" declared Tomayo. "The golden rule, you know. I am bound by it!"

"I'm afraid we don't carry it quite that

far, Doctor."

"You more than make up for it by your mercy, your tender kindness. Hospitality to the stranger is a high virtue. In Oriental countries it is considered the highest. But you must not tire yourself out for us, dear lady. You must have your sleep. To paraphrase the immortal Bard —"

The immortal Bard went unparaphrased. The door of the bedroom opened abruptly, and a man stood at the threshold. He was a short, neat man, up in his fifties. His eyes were small and sharp. Chronic impatience and an irritable severity could be read at a glance in his knotty face. He looked to be the type of cowman who, humorless as a snapping turtle, drove himself and everybody around him hard, resented anything in the nature of pleasure as a waste of precious time, and suffered dyspepsia from bolting his food too fast.

His intolerant, unfriendly eyes stabbed at Gray on the bed, at Bas Tomayo, and shifted to the girl. "Whiskey!" he rasped in a voice clipped tight from anger. "Servin' 'em whiskey! I helped lug that feller up in here, when my own judgment told me I shouldn't do it! You gonna coddle him all the rest o' the night?"

The girl, reddening with embarrassment,

said to Gray hurriedly, "This is Ira Hamp. He —"

Ira Hamp didn't let her finish. "I been lookin' the buckboard over," he went on. "It's all banged up! Where've they been with it? How'd they get hold of it?"

She raised a restraining hand to him, the weariness of her action telling plainly that Ira Hamp too often abused his privileges. "They had to borrow it. The men in town took their horses and mobbed them. That's how Captain Steel got hurt. They had to get away as best they could."

Then with a rise of anger she exclaimed, "Everybody in the Sierra Verde has gone mad, I think! A couple of travelers ride through, and without the slightest evidence they're branded as enemies! It's unjust! Outrageous! We could at least wait to find out if —"

"That don't concern me!" Ira Hamp broke in, while Bas Tomayo was wagging his head over the injustice of it all. "My concern is this outfit. I'm runnin' the roundup on a mighty tight schedule, an' I can't spare the time to be watchin' over you, Miss Anne! I can't do a good job as foreman an' do that, too!"

His use of that term — foreman — indicated that he also was originally from somewhere up North. Southwestern cowmen didn't commonly use it. The man running a Southwestern outfit was the range boss, the top screw, the high cock-a-doodle, or the ramrod. Or something casually disrespectful. Here in the Sierra Verde, despite its location, everybody seemed to have Northern roots.

"I never asked you or anybody else to watch over me," Anne Wallace retorted moderately. "You don't need to waste your time fretting over the buckboard, either."

"That's as may be," said Hamp. The damage to the buckboard was manifestly an offense to him. He was foreman and held himself importantly responsible for everything on the place. "Marley borrowed it. It was him shoulda brung it back. You ask me, they stole it off him!"

Gray spoke up. "It was a kind of swap," he said. "I took the buckboard in exchange for our horses."

"Your horses ain't none o' my concern!" Hamp snapped.

"We have returned the buckboard," Tomayo pointed out, "with thanks and apologies to Miss Wallace. You, I gather, only work here, so —"

"Shut your trap, Mex, or whatever you are!" Ira Hamp thrust out his chin. He was a man whose perceptions were low, and he failed to detect the wicked glint that instantly leaped in Tomayo's yellow eyes. "I'm just sore enough to shut it for you with my fist!"

Gray, half rising from the bed, said swiftly to Tomayo, "Hold it — hold it!" only he, not Ira Hamp or Anne Wallace, recognized the lethal significance of the little Yucatano's baleful smile, the stillness of his hands, and the soft hiss of an indrawn breath.

Anne Wallace said to the Twin Peaks foreman in chill rebuke, "I think we had better go downstairs and talk this over! You can apologize later to Dr. Maroon!"

"I ain't got time for a lot o' talk, busy as I be tryin' to keep the outfit goin' right," Hamp growled surlily as he preceded her out of the bedroom. "An' don't you look to me to apologize to anybody, least of all a greaser! I'm foreman here, an' what I say goes!"

"Easy, *amigo!*" Gray whispered to Tomayo. "Easy, now, dammit! Let him go. He's just an old fool!"

Bas Tomayo turned his smile on Gray, but it was an entirely different kind of smile, wryly forbearing.

Ira Hamp evidently did not entertain a high regard for feminine intelligence. Gray and Tomayo could hear him, going downstairs with Anne Wallace, say to her, "Gahd! I only wish Russ was here. He'd know what to do with the likes o' them two! You wimmen don't know up from down when it comes to men. Russ wouldn't put 'em up in the best bedroom if he was here, that's for sure, an' play the fool over 'em, treatin' 'em like they was high mucketty-mucks."

"That's my privilege, Ira. You forget who I am and what I am. I'm half owner of Twin Peaks, let me remind you, and I'm in charge until Russ gets back."

"All right, Miss Anne, all right! You're boss till Russ gets back. Sure! Then you'll see. Russ won't like this, I tell you now! Them two . . ."

Their voices faded away.

Gray lay back on the bed. He gazed unseeing at the ceiling.

"Her name," he said reflectively, "is Anne Wallace." He repeated it. "Anne Wallace. Nice name." He frowned, his lips drawn in a straight line. "Who is she? Russell Wallace's sister? Half owner, she said, of this Twin Peaks spread. His sister? The Judge didn't know about her. Anyhow, he didn't mention her to me when I took on this dam' job. Tomayo, you had a chance to talk with the lady before I came to, didn't you? What did you find out?"

"About her? She's not important to us. We didn't come here to —"

"I've got to know! It's important . . . a thousand times more important to me than this job!"

"A very valuable lady! To you, that is, not to me. This job is worth ten thousand dollars, plus a bonus for fast work and the war chest if we can get hold of it."

Tomayo didn't speak again for a while after that. He sat down and built a cigarette, using Gray's makings. A tiny tremor shook his fingers, and he licked his lips before running the tip of his tongue along the edge of the brown paper. He lighted the cigarette and puffed fiercely, hunched over in the chair, his eyelids half closed.

"Yes, I talked with her after we carried you in," he said at last. "She believed my story. Her manner toward me was reasonably friendly and natural, until you stared at her when she brought in the whiskey. I thought for a minute you had lost your mind! You were inexcusably rude! Judas, if I had looked at her like that, she would have snubbed me cold!"

He flung the cigarette to the floor. Its burning end burst into a shower of sparks, and he ground them out under his heel. His moods, cynically gay or broodingly vicious, changed without warning, and at times they seemingly slipped out of his control. The vicious mood was on him now. His voice was thin and unpleasantly grating.

"She lives here, and she's unmarried. She *says* she is Russell Wallace's sister and owns a share of the ranch. I can detect a Texas accent in her speech, and so can you — better than I can, no doubt. Yet Russell Wallace is definitely not a Texan! You can figure out the probable answer to that little puzzle, if you've got to know about the lady who calls herself Anne Wallace!"

Gray scowled. "Cut it out! I know Hamp riled you. He did me, too. But that's no cause for you to blackguard the girl behind her back!"

Tomayo continued talking as though he hadn't heard Gray's angry objection. "It doesn't matter who or what she is or where she came from. She's not important, except as a symbol to remind me of what *I* might have been!" A spasm of agonized self-pity contorted his tawny, delicate-featured face. "It's what *I* am that matters to me!"

He glared sullenly down at the floor. "I was cheated the day I was born! And life could have been so glorious! My father possessed wealth and breeding — and a mad devil possessed him. His was a proud family, internationally known, with Spanish rifles a mile long. He fell out with them at a family gathering, where they reprimanded him for his wild conduct. From that time on, my father deliberately did everything to embarrass and humiliate them, his own family. He publicly committed the most fantastic acts. I am the result of one of them. Weird little mongrel!"

Before such a stark revelation of concentrated bitterness, Gray could find nothing to say. Something had got Tomayo started, and he had to get it off his chest. Sweat broke out on his forehead while he sat there, huddled, glaring down the spent years into the faraway past. His voice fell to a sneering monotone.

"It amused my father to marry an Indian woman of the lowest class and flaunt the poor ignorant creature in the faces of his elegant relatives. He was delighted when she bore him a son — me. Delighted at my looks. Undersized aborigine with coyote eyes, like my mother, but having the unmistakable red hair and fine features of the haughty Tomayos! As a boy I was paraded on every occasion, dressed as a tiny *hidalgo*. Later, as part of the joke, he sent me to Europe to be educated, as the best families did their sons. I was given unlimited funds and encouraged to spend with a splash. Oh, I lived in silks!"

He giggled mirthlessly. "How I've lived since then is quite a different story. My father, curse him, made no provision for me after his death. That would have spoiled the joke. He died while I was abroad. His family took over the estate. They cut me off. Refused to recognize my existence. When my money gave out, I had to live on my wits. You think you've gone bad, Gray? Hah! You've hardly started. I've gone the full route! I've had to, to exist. Cheating and trickery, blackmail, robbery and murder — what haven't I done?"

Gray wished he would shut up. This naked exposure oddly embarrassed him. He sensed in Bas Tomayo a compulsive urge to confess, to confess in a manner that bespoke self-revulsion rather than soul-cleansing. Some burning emotion had caught up with Tomayo and fired a reaction that he could not throttle down. But he, Gray, was not his confessor, and he drew back from hearing further details of personal tragedy and crime.

"I've often found it convenient to change my name as well as my nationality," Tomayo said. He slowly pounded his knee with his small fist. "Never could I succeed in changing myself! Never! A man's whole life can be decided by an accident of birth, by his appearance, his size and shape, coloring, the arrangement of his features. . . . Everything about my appearance is abnormal, so how could I live a normal life? People are repelled by me, or they are amused. In all eyes, I see the familiar dislike, or, worse, the unforgivable insult of secret, scornful laughter. I have killed men who laughed aloud at me. And a woman or two."

He struck his knee again in futile rage. "I am a man! Yet, because of my peculiar size and incongruous coloring, I am looked upon as something less — a freak! A pariah! That girl downstairs. She was friendly to me, even respectful. Then you looked at her. She looked at you. She didn't look at me again. The comparison between us — Judas! Damn you, Gray! Damn your tall body and —"

"O.K., *amigo!*" Gray cut in. This was more comfortable ground. This abusive tangent on Tomayo's part offered a welcome return to normal talk. He asked, "Is she staying here alone, d'you happen to know?"

Tomayo shrugged and straightened up. A smile, at first wry and ghostly, then full and false, lighted his face. He wiped the beaded sweat from his forehead and spoke with almost his old tone of mocking insolence.

"Stupid question! Didn't Hamp say he is running the roundup on a tight schedule? If I judge him right, that means he has the whole crew out sweating, including the cook. His job as foreman here is more serious to him than the crack of doomsday. Russell Wallace is away somewhere, probably lining up gunhands for the Sierra Verde Pool."

"So she's alone, for the time being."

"Of course she is! That is, except for you and me. And our presence here, as Hamp warned her, would not be very likely to please, ah, brother Russ! Would it please you, if you were in his boots?"

The insinuation brought back Gray's scowl. "If I was her brother —"

"What a thought!" Tomayo scoffed. "Your look at her was anything but brotherly! By the way, what made you keep staring at her so rudely? Did you think you knew her? An old flame, perhaps?"

Avoiding answering the question, Gray said curtly, "In this country, we generally try to keep our mouth clean when we speak of decent women."

Tomayo's laugh was satiric. "Far be it from me to offend your tender sensibilities,

109

Gray, but let us be realistic! She wears a diamond bracelet. Russell Wallace is the biggest rancher in the Upper Pecos. He is single. Well-to-do bachelors occasionally take lovely ladies under their, ah, protection and install them in their homes, passing them off as their housekeeper, or a cousin, or whatever seems plausible. I don't say that is the case here, mind you —"

"Then why don't you drop it?" Gray snapped.

"However," Tomayo pursued tranquilly, "let Russell Wallace get word that some male guests are sharing his house with the lady and I wager he'll come heading home in a hurry! I hope I'm right. Then we can capture him and wind up this job."

He stared thoughtfully at Gray. "You didn't answer my question. That's your privilege. But your eyes have been giving you away while I talked about the lady! You *have* known her before! Or —"

"Shut up, damn you!"

"— Or you think you've known her. She crossed your life at some time. Or someone very much like her. You're not sure. Therefore, she must have used a different name. And I don't suppose she had a brother. Ah, well! We all change. Beauty, too, must make its bargains with —"

Gray started up from the bed. "I'll shut your mouth if I have to choke you!"

"Never mind," Tomayo murmured. "It doesn't matter to me what she is. She's not important."

9
No Retreat

Gray released a sigh. The hard mask settled over his face, a face scarred by too many fights and etched with lines that had come too soon for his years. Life, he reflected bleakly, was nothing better than a desert trail attended by an endless procession of mirages, each shimmering mirage fading away as it was approached. Even with all his experience, he could still be gulled along, wanting to believe, his faith captured until his cup dipped dry sand, then on to the next bright illusion.

And yet. . . . *Whatever she is,* ran an unbidden thread of thought, *I'm caught! This time I can't go on!*

He brushed aside the private confession to himself, half refusing to accept it. "What shape am I in?" he asked Tomayo.

"The sheriff's bullet seems to have grazed the bone as well as a tendon in your lower thigh," Tomayo answered. "That accounts for the numbness in your leg. The other bullet could easily have knocked the parietal bone askew in your cranium, if you hadn't fortunately been as thick-skulled as I suspected. It fluked and parted your hair rather prettily on the side."

"You handle the lingo like a surgeon, all right, I'll grant that."

"You should have seen the impressive performance I put on for Anne Wallace's benefit! She's a darling. I quite outdid myself. When the stiffness leaves your leg, there's no reason why you shouldn't be up and around. You'll have a limp for a while and a bit of a headache, perhaps, but on the whole you got off lucky."

"Soon as I can," Gray stated with sudden resolution, "I'm getting out of here, Wallace or no Wallace! Got to! Tomorrow! Today! Past midnight, isn't it? Today, yes!"

Tomayo took a turn up and down the bedroom, fingering his lips and shooting narrowed glances at Gray. "You won't do any such insane thing!"

"Who says I won't?"

"I do! You're my patient, remember, and I forbid it!"

"The hell with that! You said —"

Tomayo made a dismissing pass with his

hand. "I have just now held a professional consultation with my better self and reversed my previous opinion. You stay there! I hung your guns and belts up there on the wall. They're out of your reach. If necessary, I'll give you a medicinal tap on the skull with one of mine when you're not looking, and you'll have a very sudden relapse!"

"Why, dam' your nerve! You take orders from me —"

"Listen, Gray!" Tomayo halted at the foot of the bed. It was without thought or intention, perhaps, that he brought his right hand to rest on his holster. "For your own good as well as mine, listen! Whatever's weighing on your mind, forget it! We have a job to do here. We can't back out. His Honor gave the orders, and you know what it would mean to go against him! I can see you going in empty-handed and telling him, 'We got to Twin Peaks. We were in Wallace's house. But he was out, and we didn't wait!' I can see His Honor's face! 'Yes, we walked right out of Wallace's house, because there was a girl there who —' "

"Leave her out of it, I tell you!"

"Sorry, no can do! I see now she *is* important and she *does* matter! You're not thinking straight because of her. You want us to throw up the job. Because of her! That makes her damned important to me!" Tomayo laughed soundlessly, watching Gray's face. "Wallace will be back. It will be soon, if he hears of our being here. I suppose he keeps in touch with the outfit, wherever he goes, seeing he's owner. We will be here waiting for him!"

"And what about Marley and the Trail Fork crowd? They're bound to learn we're here."

"True. Hamp will tell them, first chance he gets, and they'll come for us — unless darling Anne prevails on Hamp to keep quiet. But if they do come, and she stands up for us, what then? They'd hardly drag us out, or even try, over her protests. She's part owner here, and she ranks as mistress of this house we're in! She's our ace! In fact, I begin to feel that she's the one good card we have. Oh, yes, she matters. Yes, indeed. And we can make very good use of her!"

"Hide behind a girl's skirts?" Gray inquired, trying to lacerate the little man's warped vanity.

But Tomayo nodded, unabashed. "Why not? I imagine she has a lot of spirit. She would go all out for any man who won her trust and respect and loyalty. Excellent qualities, those. They can usually be aroused in a woman, I have observed, through one dominant emotion — love. I admit, regretfully, that I do not possess the personal qualifications to insure success with the lady. So that's your job! Right?"

"Wrong!" Gray growled at him, thinking he was joking.

Tomayo helped himself to a drink from the whiskey bottle on the tray, remarking that it was a poor doctor who wouldn't take a dose of his own prescription. "Gray, you're a fool!" he said coolly. "A thick-headed fool! I saw how you looked at her. And for just an instant she looked at you in the same manner. Exactly the same! You caught her off guard. I'm not blind. She's already attracted to you, strongly attracted. The rest should be easy for you."

Gray stared at him, realizing that he meant it, incredulous at the cold-blooded gall of the man.

"What could be more natural?" Tomayo argued. "She is alone. Lonely. Wallace is away. Along you come, a tall man, not old, passably presentable in a rough fashion. You're hurt, needing her tender care. You're a lonely sort of fool, too, and you give her a virile look, which she instinctively returns! She is passion and fire and affection, gorgeously beautiful, feminine . . . oh, hell!"

He swung away, restlessly finger-combing his monstrous shock of red hair. When next he spoke, he pitched his voice low and flat.

"All right, *Señor Lobo,* go ahead and walk out of it! Go on back to Blakeville! Tell His Honor, when you get there, that little Basilio is sticking to the job until it's finished! I'll get it done alone somehow, I swear! There's too much in it for me to throw away. The money, for one thing."

He looked suddenly aged, wearily satanic, a man who had plumbed the blackest depths of crime. "Money is all that matters," he muttered, leaving the room. "Damn everything else!"

Tomayo stayed absent the rest of the night and did not show up in the morning. Ordinarily, Gray would have shrugged it off as fairly typical of him, having noticed that he never seemed to need much sleep and was as nocturnal in his habits as a tomcat. Since last night's rift, though, there was a danger that he would try to play a lone hand and raise mischief. Anne Wallace did not inquire about him, from which Gray surmised that he was still on the ranch, or else had given her some plausible reason for his absence. Gray couldn't ask her without letting her wonder what was amiss between her two uninvited guests.

Not until the afternoon did Tomayo put in an appearance, his manner airily self-assured. He raised his eyebrows when Gray neither spoke nor glanced at him.

Gray was staring blankly at the ceiling, like a man in a state of catalepsy, a question thudding over and over in his mind: *Is she — ?*

Anne Wallace had brought him his meals, had later come in to remove the dishes, had lingered. Her visits had built up in him a flood of feeling, had placed an unbearable strain on him.

He could recall and hear again her every word, every inflection of her voice. Every slightest motion. He could see her. Sunlight through the window brought out rich under-tones of her dark hair so that they glowed alive like deep fires. It struck further fires in her emerald eyes and caused a faintly blue shadow to appear under the curve of her throat when she bent her head.

When she arranged the tray on the bed, her nearness forced him to draw back from her, dismayed at what it did to him and not trusting his own involuntary actions. It was useless trying to remind himself that she might very likely be here under false pre-tenses and a false name, with all the loss of womanly honor that that implied. His senses ignored it. This time the mirage persisted and swiftly grew more real. A shred of cynical reason warned that there was no substance beneath the vision, that it must disintegrate and vanish like the others in barren disillusion. In his heart he wished to stay hoodwinked.

As she bent over him, her long eyelashes lay softly against her cheeks, almost brushing them, as if to conceal her eyes, and her features showed only a cool composure. Then she smiled, and her expression was lighted by a warm and lovely frankness that said silently, "I'm so glad you are here."

That look haunted Gray. It took him searching back in recollection over the years, but a memory that for long had stayed vivid was now blurred. He found that he could not quite recapture it. The face of Anne Wallace intervened.

Is she — ?

"How's the suffering patient today?" inquired Tomayo, flicking ash from a good cigar that he had purloined from somewhere on the premises. "You have decided to wait for brother Russell after all, eh? Too bad! I looked forward to earning ten thousand dollars all for myself, plus a bonus and whatever valuable perquisites I could get away

118

with from here!"

Gray stirred, forsaking his visions. He eyed Tomayo narrowly, paying sharp examination to what he had said. "I'd as soon leave her here alone with a Yaqui cutthroat, as with you!"

"Oho! The protective male instinct!" Tomayo clicked his tongue. "I see you've taken your guns down off the wall. That look on your face as I came in — oh, you've got it hard!" He leered like a copper satyr. "And the eyes of darling Anne do softly shine with a pensiveness that only a blind man could miss seeing. Accept my congratulations, Captain Steel. You worked fast, and so did she, if 'work' is the right word. I am sure you will both enjoy much happiness."

Resisting the urge to hurl a boot at him, Gray asked him bluntly, "What did you mean, 'valuable perquisites'? If you mean the war chest, say so. If you mean *her* — drop it! I wouldn't put it past you to try taking her down to Blakeville, if Wallace doesn't show up!"

"That thought has occurred to me," Tomayo admitted blandly. "A substitute in place of Wallace. Half success in place of failure. His Honor would pay a reward, if her abduction were done very secretly. Having her as hostage, he would have a hold

119

over Wallace, wouldn't he? No doubt Wallace prizes her as highly as you do. However" — he waggled a reassuring hand — "that is not my plan at present."

"Your plan? Yours?" Gray's tone was dangerously quiet and gentle. "Little man, are you trying to take charge?"

He was conscious of the alteration in relationship between himself and Tomayo this day. Where, up until last night, Tomayo's insolence had been lightly impersonal and even humorous, now it contained a steel core. He was as flippant as ever, but he was not joking.

There had developed between them something that approached a give-and-take understanding, arising from their hazardous situation and desperate mission. Today it existed in form, not in content. Perhaps Tomayo regretted having gone that far toward friendship. He was friendless by choice and by circumstances, a renegade who jeered at all mankind and allowed nothing to interfere with his credo of solitary self-interest.

At Gray's biting question, Tomayo let his smile fade. His yellow eyes stilled, drained of every trace of humor, and for a bare instant corrosive malice glinted in them.

"Not at all," he murmured. "The little

man knows his humble place!" A muscle quivered above one eye. He continued referring strangely to himself in the third person. "His place is merely that of your helper. Your little helper. His Honor ordered the funny little man — the freakish little Mex —"

"Forget it!" Gray said uncomfortably. "I didn't call you all that. Tell me what you've got in mind and quit being so blasted touchy!"

"Yes, master. Your wish is my command, master. I have the honor to serve you, master, and that is my sole function." Tomayo's expression was a mask of exaggerated humility that thinly overlaid a sneer. "Ira Hamp rode in again today from the roundup camp," he related in the tone of a lowly serf addressing a feudal baron. "He talked for some time with Anne — excuse me, sir, I mean Miss Wallace, your hostess."

Irritated by his elaborate pose and unnecessary pauses, Gray demanded, "Well, what of it?"

"I was able to overhear their conversation. The roundup is going well, and camp is being moved farther back in the hills, north."

"It's a big range Twin Peaks uses, I guess, and rough in spots — piñon and juniper where it isn't brush and rocks."

"There has been a letter from Russell Wallace. From Texas." Tomayo dropped the farce, evidently tiring of it. "Our guess about him was only half correct," he said crisply. "He's over in the Panhandle. On behalf of the Sierra Verde Pool — and we know, of course, he is the head of it — his task is to raise a company of warhands as fast as he can. A whole company, mind you, of ex-Rangers and discharged soldiers and the like! Experienced fighting men, fully armed and equipped, organized under his command! The company is to be known as the Sierra Verde Vigilantes, presumably to give it a semiofficial touch. A lot of money is being poured into the war chest to pay for it."

"How many men is Wallace out to hire?"

"Between eighty and a hundred, I believe. That's what I heard mentioned, anyway."

"Phew!" Gray whistled softly. "A lot of scrappers for a cowman to boss. Too many."

"Brother Russ," Tomayo drawled, "knows what he is doing, I fancy. Unlike you, he *did* hold the rank of Army captain. And, again unlike you, he fought on the Union side. I wonder," he said with affected innocence, "why his sister has that Texas accent?"

Gray winced, scowled, and reverted to the main subject. "With eighty good men, not counting the cattle crowd, Wallace could stand off the Judge. He could even ride down to Blakeville and settle things once and for all! The Judge better get a move on and do something quick or he's a gone duck!"

"I thought that was what we were here for. Or are you backing out?" Tomayo was being deliberately disagreeable. "It wouldn't be enough for them merely to stand off His Honor. They couldn't afford to support such an army forever. They intend to settle matters at one blow. And that would finish all of us, especially you! How they would love to blast down the notorious Lobo Gray, top gun of Blakeville! Or string him up, if they caught him alive! You don't realize how you are hated from one end of the Pecos to the other!"

"I guess I do," Gray said. But he hadn't, not fully, and he felt a shudder crawl down his body.

Tomayo shook his head, smiling glacially. "There are men, broken by His Honor's orders, who hate you more than they hate him — because you're the one who bossed the crew, while they rarely saw him! You have the stamp of a cowman, so every cowman who has ever heard of you curses you for a renegade, a cowman who, for a crooked politician's pay, turned against his own kind! And the blood-curdling deeds credited to you — well, they don't spoil in the telling! What a reputation! You're as much an outcast as I am, yet you talk as if you could throw up this job and walk off with a clean slate! I'll never be able to afford to have scruples, and neither will you!"

"All right, let it be." Gray's voice sounded thick and harsh. "Let it be, Tomayo. We're two of a kind, then."

The Yucatano looked at him queerly. "Two of a kind," he murmured and shrugged. "Two corpses, if Wallace's plans go through! Territory law is spread very thin, and I doubt if it would pry too earnestly into the killing of you and me and a few other undesirable citizens. And if His Honor got smashed by Wallace, there would be few tears shed over him. He must have plenty of political enemies who fear him, quite possibly the governor among them. They would be grateful to Wallace, after it was done, and have him and his men solemnly appointed special deputies or something of the kind. In politics these days it's dog eat dog, justice on the side of the winner, and devil take the hindmost. We must stop Wallace, not only for Judge Blake's sake — and for the reward — but to save our own skins!

I say *we* had better get a move on and get something done!"

Gray granted the accuracy of Tomayo's statement of the case. Territory politics, tangled in elective offices, government appointments, and military controls, was a jungle of intrigue. Once a powerful politico slipped and fell, the rest trampled over him.

It had been so, more or less, ever since the Mexican War, when the somewhat infamous General Armijo fled before General Kearney's far-marching U. S. troops, leaving his mantle of supreme authority behind to be squabbled over. There was plenty of scope in the Territory for private wars and feuds, and its politics were occasionally clouded in powder smoke here and there. The problem of the Spanish and Mexican land grants had never been settled, and there existed chronic dissatisfaction among the old owners and their heirs, who supported any candidate promising to use his dubious influence in helping to restore to them their family estates — vast tracts of land that had lain mostly uninhabited from time immemorial. The same candidates stoutly promised new homesteaders more land and free titles, at the same time vowing to the cattlemen that the range would be kept open for them. Only the most nimble politician could reconcile those three awkward issues while at the same time solving the problem of sheep.

"Two of us to stop a whole cockeyed army of shooters!" Gray reflected aloud. "This thing doesn't get any easier!"

Tomayo gave his hat an upthrust and folded his arms. "Before Hamp left here today, he went into the ranch office with Miss Wallace," he reported. "It's in a small building set apart from the house, on the east side, the side opposite to the bunkhouse. It is kept locked, and there is a steel safe in there, an old-fashioned one. I had a look at it through the window. Miss Wallace has the keys — she opened it for Hamp to put away a tally book. I think the war chest is there."

"You appear to have done considerable spying around the place," Gray remarked.

"My ears and eyes have not been idle. Wallace has established a camp on the Muleshoe, just over the Texas line. A sort of temporary field headquarters, where he is recruiting and organizing his company. When he is ready, practically every able cowman hereabouts is expected to join in. They are determined to force a quick showdown, that is obvious, but not until roundup is over. That explains Hamp's hurry. Every outfit in the Sierra Verde is rushing to get finished."

Gray nodded. "A cowman's work can't be put off, once it's begun. And those Union hotshots generally tried to get everything set just right before they jumped. It gives us a breathing spell." He had a thought. "You don't reckon Wallace took the war chest with him?"

"No. As far as I could learn, they had only raised part of it when he left. I think it is in the safe."

"Then he may have to come home soon for some of the money. Running a big camp is expensive, and the men have to be paid."

"He may, but can we depend on it? No." Tomayo put his fingertips delicately together, making a steeple of them. "Can we break off the spearpoint? Yes!" His fingers curled inward. "By snatching that war chest! It would at least delay them until they could raise more money. Dutifully warned by us, His Honor would have time to call in all his men and make the first move. Strike first and strike hard! He has no choice left. It is a matter of survival. And we are the ones best fitted to lead His Honor's enforcers up here and take over the Sierra Verde, while Wallace and his vigilantes are stewing in

Texas! Yes, if we can steal their war chest . . ."

"I'm not exactly for it," Gray said shortly. "Maybe I'm all you say I am, but I don't go in for robbing a place where I — uh — where I'm a guest."

"Scruples!" Tomayo jeered. "Well, there is no guarantee that we would find it in the safe, so that is another chance we can't depend on, isn't it? Probably the surest and quickest plan, after all, is the one involving Anne Wallace! You don't approve of that, either."

"I sure don't!"

"You object to everything. She will be alone here with us the rest of the day, with not another soul on the place, and she has the key to the safe! There are good horses in one of the corrals and spare saddles in the wagon shed. It would be simple to take her off after dark — and if we do find the war chest in the safe, so much the better! She need not be hurt, only frightened. By riding hard all night, we can be in Blakeville with her in the morning. What is there to stop us?"

Gray said, "Me!" He slid his legs out of the bed and stood up.

"Oh, you're in shape to ride. See, you can

use that leg now. You may bleed a bit, but —"

"That's not what I mean." Gray dragged his gun belts out from underneath the bed-covers. "Here's my meaning, Tomayo. I'd kill any man who tried it! *Any* man! Is that plain enough for you?"

They stared unblinking at each other. In a sinister mood, Tomayo seemed to ponder on whether or not to take up the challenge. Reaching a decision, he picked up his half-smoked cigar from the tray, inspected it thoughtfully, found it dead, and dropped it. He reached over for the whiskey bottle, filled a glass to the brim, and downed it in a single gulp without a flinch.

"You'll never live to see the day —" he began, and stopped as if the phrase was one that might convey more than he intended saying. His smile came, more shallow and false than ever, not diminishing the chill of his eyes.

"Very well, *Señor Lobo!* Then that's out . . . as far as you are concerned!" He seemed actually relieved at having brought about an open clash in which they could declare themselves at cross-purposes. "The longer we wait, the more risks we run, and you are not in the best shape to pull a fast shoot-out and a getaway. This is too good to last.

It will go bad very soon. You can be caught in it, but not me! I shall use my own resources to get this job done!"

He moved to the door. "Is that plain enough for *you?*" he purred and minced out, softly whistling a cheerless little dirge through his teeth.

Gray narrowed his eyes at the closing door. The manner as much as the words of his little helper carried a clear notice that he was ready to double-cross Gray and leave him in the lurch. Discarding subtlety for once, along with any pretense that he was to be trusted, Tomayo was choosing to expose himself at his worst, as a man who hadn't the shadow of a conscience left in his sin-steeped soul. He could stand up to an armed mob, or he could knife a partner in the back — whichever the occasion called for — equally without a qualm.

Some other words that Tomayo had uttered, leaving the sentence unfinished, stirred up a hazy recollection that Gray strove to capture and examine: *"You'll never live to see the day —"*

He connected those words with the racing buckboard in Trail Fork, with his head wound and the blinding white flash in his eyes. They had something to do with the Judge.

For an instant, he almost caught the connection. It was so close he knew it as a thought that he'd had at that time. An icy bit of revelation. But he was trying too hard, and it slipped away from him like a dim and dreamlike figment of the imagination.

He shook his head, shoving the guns and shell-studded belts back under the bedcovers. He knew all there was to know about the Judge, and if the lost thought concerned him, it could not have been as important as he felt it was.

The important thing was that Tomayo had the itch to do the job by any means at his disposal, no matter how foul, before the risks piled up and exploded. In the event that Russell Wallace remained unavailable, Anne was second best as hostage, and in his present satanic temper, Tomayo would not hesitate to take her and the war chest, if he could work it.

That thought of Tomayo handing Anne over to the Judge conjured up an intolerable vision that Gray thrust away. The solution, he guessed, was to go and capture Russell Wallace on the Muleshoe. Or steal the war chest, provided it was here.

Or kill Tomayo.

10
LOOT

The moon that night slanted a steady light through the window and bleached the bedroom's earlier darkness to a pale, silver-shot gloom in which all the furniture became visible. The door swung inward, casting an oblong shadow over the side wall. The shadow bulged, and Tomayo slipped noiselessly into the room. He looked at the bed. It was empty.

"Don't you sleep anymore?" Gray inquired of him dryly.

Fully dressed and wearing his gun belts, he stepped from behind the opened door. He had moved there from the window, seconds ahead of Tomayo's entrance. He dipped a glance at Tomayo's hands, half expecting to see a knife. When his trust ran out, it ran out all the way.

Tomayo didn't miss that glance. A slight tightening, barely perceptible, thinned his lips. A flare started in his eyes and died. To Gray's query he responded, "Not tonight."

"Nor me," Gray said. He nodded in the direction of the front of the house. "I heard riders come in about an hour after sundown. You seen them?"

"Of course." It was Tomayo's turn to inspect Gray's hands, and he did it deliberately. "I have seen them before. So have you. In the saloon in Trail Fork. One of them is that big-mouthed fool Marley. The other is the lanky one who spoke up — Scanlon, Anne Wallace called him. They went into the ranch office, talking about money, the Pool, and brother Russ. They lighted a lamp and shut the door. I tried to peer in, but Marley pulled a drape over the window. Some people are so suspicious they —"

"Must be that something has come up. Serious, maybe. Did you hear us mentioned?"

"I have told you what I heard. It was not much. I shall try again now, and if I have to I'll —"

"No," Gray said. "I'll take it this time."

He had not meant to speak the words in curt command, but because of distrust his voice was crisp and hard. He was thinking that Tomayo's purpose in entering the bedroom so quietly had not been merely to offer him a small dab of news. Thinking, too, that it wouldn't do to let Tomayo go back down on his own, perhaps to kill Marley and Scanlon. It wouldn't do at all. It was time to jerk the reins up on him.

Tomayo inclined his head, in hollow sham

of humbleness, hiding whatever was in his eyes. "I shall wait here for you, then . . . needless to say, with bated breath!"

The bedroom opened onto an upstairs hallway that had a carpeted staircase at the end toward the front of the house — rare among ranch houses, but this was a Northern-style home, unusually large and elaborate. No lights showed anywhere except from the crack beneath the closed door of a downstairs front room.

Gray descended the stairs to the main hallway, limped through it, and drew open the front door. Instead of a raised porch, there was a portico at ground level, flag-stoned — a Mexican touch that somehow lent itself harmoniously to the otherwise thoroughly North American style of the house. Two saddled horses, their cinches loosened, dozed at the hitchrack beyond the flagstones.

On the east side of the house, Tomayo had said, was the ranch office. Gray turned that way, came to the end of the portico, and there it was, a small, squat building shaded by aged cottonwoods. Probably the original ranch house, before prosperity made pos-sible the big two-story house that now over-lorded the yard. Subdued lamplight seeped through a draped window of the tree-shadowed building.

Leaving the portico, Gray crossed the moonlit yard, trod carefully under the cottonwoods to the closed door, and stood there motionless, listening to voices in the office. The act of eavesdropping, minor as it was compared to the purpose that had brought him to Twin Peaks, provoked in him a twinge of shame. He reminded himself that if he didn't do it, Tomayo would.

The closed door and draped window muffled the talk. He crept closer until, with his ear to the door, he could distinguish the words being spoken. It was easy to pick out Marley's heavy, rasping voice.

"Takes a pile more'n we first figured," Marley was saying. "Sure, everybody's chipping in best they can. No holdouts, an' they'll be ready when Russ is, soon's branding's done. They wouldn't if it wasn't him, though. An' that goes for me, too, I'll admit. We're gambling an awful lot on him, an' we can't afford to lose!"

A more modulated but dry voice, that of the lanky Scanlon, queried, "Can any of us afford *not* to gamble on him, John? We've got to back him straight through, or else give in to Judge Blake — and you know what that would mean! New laws and high taxes! Graft! Gangs of gunmen flashing badges and arrest warrants! Cousin of mine, down the Lower Pecos, had his place seized for a delinquent tax bill he'd never heard of. There was a rigged auction, and he got sold out for thirty dollars. Carpetbag tactics — here in the Territory, where most of us went Union! Person'ly, I'll gamble my last dollar to keep Judge Blake out of the Sierra Verde! You won't hear me griping what it costs!"

"Now, Frank, you know I'm not griping," Marley grumbled. "You know I've put in my share. I only say Russ's letter doesn't tell all I'd like to know. It's too short."

"Want him to write it down every time he spits and how the weather's there?"

"You make the jokes. I'm too worried. Some o' the fellers keep coming round asking me how Russ is doing this an' doing that, like I should know. Can I see his letter again, Anne? Like to read it over."

There was an assenting murmur from Anne Wallace. Gray bent closer against the door, trying to ease the strain on his injured leg, and caught a few of her words: ". . . in a day or two . . . tell you himself . . ."

"Good thing," Marley said. "It's a pile of money to be holding here — close to thirty thousand dollars. I guess that's a hefty safe, though."

"Took a crew with tackle to put it there," commented Scanlon. "I freighted it in for his father, way before the War. He bought it cheap from a busted bank up in Raton. You couldn't dent it with a sledge hammer. Don't add the money to your worries, John. That's the safest safe . . . *huh?*"

Gray's injured leg, held braced too long under his bent position, had got a cramp in it. In straightening up quickly to remedy it by kicking out, Gray was forced momentarily to increase his weight on it. His knee buckled. He lurched off balance, and his elbow bumped the door.

"Huh?" Scanlon exclaimed again. "Was that your foot, John?"

"It sure wasn't!" A chair scraped noisily, and hard heels hit the floor. "Somebody outside trying to get in!"

Any chance of darting off under the cottonwood shadows was hopeless. Gray stooped, holding his aching knee in his hands and working the cramp out of it. It occurred to him that it might have been better to let Tomayo do the spying.

Whatever faults Marley had, timid inactivity was not one of them. Forthright and gun in hand, he jerked open the door of the ranch office and all but collided with Gray.

"Evenin'," Gray said. With the lamplight

shining on him, he continued massaging his knee, keeping his head lowered. "Coffee on?"

Full of the notion of charging forth into the night in pursuit of a prowler, Marley hauled up short and blinked down at the stooping figure before him. All Gray saw of the cowman was a pair of thick legs. He hoped he wasn't going to have to see more.

"What the blazes you doing?"

"Getting a sore kink out o' my leg."

Marley, his train of thought lumbering at the switch, said, "Oh," with perfunctory sympathy. Rough horses could wear down the gristle in any range rider's joints. But further cogitation found the reply inadequate to his question. "I mean what're you doing *here*?"

"Looking for the cook shack."

"Oh," said Marley again, satisfied. "It's over the other side o' the house, cowboy. Doubt there's any coffee on, though, 'cause Hamp put the cook on the chuck wagon, y'know."

"That's right. Forgot." Gray made to hobble off, still rubbing his knee. "Reckon I'll turn in. 'Night."

"'Night."

It was Scanlon, shoving past Marley at the door, who said sharply, "Wait a minute!"

His legs scissored a long stride and stopped. "*Wait — a — minute!* Who're you that you don't know your way round here? Let's see your face!"

Gray halted, letting his hands dangle. Slowly, he raised his eyes to the two cowmen's waists, their chests, and looked into the muzzle of a .44 leveled in Scanlon's fist.

Scanlon breathed incredulously, "Well, for — !" Shock threw harsh volume into his voice then. "Don't move! Not a blink! Know him, John? Get your gun out, you fool!"

Marley had holstered his gun. He gulped, grabbed it out, and then Gray was looking into the muzzles of two .44's. Marley's florid big face had changed color, and his gun clicked to full cock, his forefinger tightening on the trigger. Convulsive reaction was about to trip the hammer, Gray knew, and he was within a wink of making the fastest draw of his life when Anne Wallace cried out frantically, "Don't shoot — he's a friend!"

Marley looked dumbly astonished, but Scanlon rapped in an iron voice, "He's *what?*"

"A friend! He's Captain Steel! He's hurt — you can see he's hurt!"

"Friend? Him?" Scanlon kept his unwavering glare on Gray. "Godamighty, Anne, you don't know what you're saying! He ain't hurt a particle to what he did in Trail Fork! Him and a pint-size Mexican! They like to've wrecked the town!"

"Blakeville gunmen!" blurted Marley. He stared beyond Gray, searching for yellow eyes in the shadows. "Blakeville gunmen, or I'm crazy! We all know 'em! We all know what they are! They showed it!"

"You're both crazy!" the girl accused them furiously. "As crazy as the rest! Captain Steel was brought here, injured and unconscious, by his friend Dr. Maroon, in our buckboard —"

"Your buckboard?" Marley broke in. "The one I borrowed? I told you it was stolen out of Trail Fork, didn't I? You didn't tell me —"

"I'm telling you now! They didn't steal it! You and the rest stole their horses and attacked them because they were strangers — no other reason! You were probably drinking, but that doesn't excuse you for behaving like a pack of madmen! They had to borrow the buckboard to escape, and they brought it here where it belongs. Is that stealing?"

Marley stabbed a finger at Gray. "If you'd seen him smash it into us! If you'd seen him in the Union Bar, him an' that Mex — !"

"If you all hadn't been drunk!"

"We were as cold sober as —"

"Then you don't have any excuse at all," Anne Wallace stormed on, adding with feminine logic, "and you should have taken better care of our buckboard, Mr. Marley! It's not your property! I think even Ira Hamp realizes the right of it, only he's too cantankerous to admit it."

Gray didn't say anything. Under the restriction of the cocked guns, it was more than difficult for him to disguise the dark hardness of his face beneath the strip of white bandage that they could now see below his hat brim. The best he could do was to keep still, as long as the argument was reduced to the question of the buckboard; and Anne Wallace was attending to that.

Scanlon broadened the matter by bursting out, "Look at him, Anne! His face! His eyes! Can't you tell what he is? Can't you *see* him?"

"I see Captain Walter Steel, a guest here on Twin Peaks!"

"Captain, huh? Lord, a woman'll believe any lie a man tells her! What outfit was he with?"

Gray said tersely, "Texas Brigade," and in Anne's quick lift of her chin, he recognized an impulsive salute. She was definitely Texan.

"A rebel!" Scanlon said. "You're on the wrong range, Reb! What were you up to, prowling here at the door?"

"He has already told you!" Anne answered for Gray. "It's his first time downstairs since we carried him into the house. How was he to know this isn't the cook shack? He saw the light on and came here. You believed him when you first opened the door, and there's no earthly reason for you to disbelieve him now!"

"B-but — !" Marley spluttered, and Scanlon cut in with, "Now look, Anne — !"

It was as far as they got. "Prowling, indeed!" she interrupted them both. "Is that what you call it when a man comes up and knocks on the door? You heard him knock! Would he have knocked if he was prowling? It's as silly as accusing him of stealing the buckboard!"

Scanlon muttered impotently, "Hell!" in an undertone, and twisted his ear with his fingers. "It wasn't a knock we heard, exactly. Not a reg'lar knock. More like —"

"Oh, for heaven's sake! Talk, talk, talk!" Anne stepped between him and Marley. "You say a woman will believe any lie a man tells her, but you men can talk yourselves right into believing any silly thing!"

She put her hands over their drawn guns and pushed them down, as token that her unassailable reasoning concluded the matter and left no further room for dispute. "Men!" she sighed resignedly . . . softly, looking at Gray.

Seeing that he might move now without getting shot, Gray raised his hat to her. Ignoring the two glowering cowmen, he said, "Sorry I blundered, Miss Anne. I seem to've been doing it since I hit these parts."

"No, they are the blunderers."

"Good night." He held her eyes with his for a moment.

Her color heightened. She smiled. "Good night."

Marley swung slowly around, keeping Gray faced as he went by. Scanlon drew his breath in and let it gush out of him with a long throaty grunt. But Anne's eyes said that the two men didn't stand a chance, that their angry suspicions were weak reeds against her impregnable faith. She might even end by making them feel that they owed apologies to Captain Walter Steel, late of the Texas Brigade, and to Dr. Euclides Maroon, distinguished surgeon from parts unknown.

Limping steadily on to the house, Gray

listened for sounds behind him. What he heard was a wild howl and a yipping, far away in the hills, drifting down with the night breeze that swept over the Sierra Verde.

"And good night to *you,* brother coyote!" he whispered.

11
THE MARAUDERS

Tomayo was in the upstairs bedroom when Gray returned. He had not waited there the whole time, however, for his first words to Gray were, "You *blundered,* all right! You never spoke truer words! Judas, how you blundered!"

"Spied on me, did you?" Gray groped to the washstand. He poured cold water into the basin from the pitcher and splashed his face. "Tomayo, let me tell you right now, I like you less and less!"

"It's mutual, probably contagious. I hate to see luck wasted on a fool. I never trust to luck. I dare not. Luck is no friend of mine; if it was, I would not be what I am. I have to depend exclusively on myself, on my talents and wits. But you can go your blundering way into the worst bungle, and luck pulls you through!"

"If I was lucky, I wouldn't get into any jackpots in the first place."

"If the luscious lady had not stood up for you, you would never have got out of that one! Luck! Did you learn anything worthwhile before you barged into that door like a blind camel?"

Gray slumped onto the bed. He was not sorry that the moonlight on the bedroom window had dimmed with the slanting ascent of the moon. He did not want Tomayo to be able to study his face too closely, and he said with feigned coolness, "You figured right about the money."

"Ah!" Tomayo lighted a cigar. The brief flare of the match showed his expression to be keenly alert, as if he hung on Gray's every word and weighed it for truth. "In the safe!"

"Wallace" — Gray's tone involuntarily hardened on the name — "will be coming for it, maybe in a couple of days."

"Can we wait?"

"You know we can't. Not here. Marley and Scanlon will spread the word."

Tomayo blew a smoke ring. He blew a smoke ball through it. "Your enchanting Anne has the key to the safe!"

"I've made my say about that!"

"I merely mentioned it to test your, ah, steadfastness — another word for stubbornness. You are paying her your allegiance, as it were, although she already has an active protector in Russell Wallace — while at the same time you are here as her enemy, under false colors! It is a curious situation, full of contradictions, largely your fault, not mine!"

"Who's blaming you?"

"The question is, what are we going to do? Yes, *we!* I can't see either of us succeeding while we are at loggerheads, so let us compromise our differences. We must not lay a hand on her, you say. Very well, I agree to that. Do you agree that we must capture the war chest?"

Gray nodded. "Providing there's any way to do it without —"

"Oh, but there is! The key is not important, really." In the semidarkness Tomayo's eyes glimmered with amusement and triumph. "That safe, so impressively massive! That poor old can! What would you bet that I couldn't spring the lock in ten minutes with a buttonhook?"

"Ten dollars. Twenty."

Tomayo chuckled. "Done! It's an old Whitehead safe. I've cracked a dozen like it, and without interference from you, I'll crack this one! It is a simple trick that even you could learn, if you put your mind to it."

"I'll learn watching you operate, Dr. Maroon."

"You're coming? But —"

"Damn right I'm coming!"

"Hmm! Tonight, then. After Marley and Scanlon leave and sweet Anne goes to bed . . ."

But Marley and Scanlon put up their horses and spent the night in the ranch office, taking with them their rifles from the saddle scabbards. They locked the door and didn't show a light.

Nor did they evince any intention of leaving the next morning; they sat on the front portico of the house, smoking, rifles beside them, backs to the wall, warily on guard. It was plain that Anne had not entirely succeeded in convincing them, or perhaps they had talked together through the night and fed each other's distrust.

Ira Hamp rode in not long after breakfast, and the two walked with him down to the corrals for a private powwow. Judging from the foreman's gesticulations, Marley and Scanlon were reviving his acrimony against Gray and Tomayo. The three of them began nodding and glancing back at the house, aligning their male sagacity against the opinion of a mere woman.

"They're not leaving while we're here, that's sure," Gray told Tomayo. "More likely they'll call in help to stand watch till Wallace gets here."

"There will be a gathering of watchdogs, yes," Tomayo agreed. "And methinks our young hostess will not be able to muzzle them. They'll be at our throats!"

"We might's well pull out right now while we can."

"I'm sure they will be happy to see us go. They are busy men. It will leave them free to get back to branding their precious cows. I have never stooped to doing work of that kind, but presumably it affords its practitioners a sense of accomplishment. Let us say our farewells. You and I do not fit in here. Let us depart forever and ease their minds."

"I guess we can borrow horses."

"Undoubtedly. And tonight, of course, we will return here for something we left behind! We can be out of the country with it ahead of the hullabaloo tomorrow, and if we are not seen, they won't even know for certain who took it! Good joke on them, eh?"

"Leave it to you to think o' that, Don Tomato!" Gray said dourly.

Tomayo flickered a cynical smile. "I followed your thought, *Señor Lobo!*"

There was a look in Anne's eyes that wasn't quite laughter, as Gray approached her; a lifting, lighthearted joyousness, as if special and wonderful news had come to her.

The look died in frank dismay when Gray made his announcement to her that he and Dr. Maroon were leaving Twin Peaks. "Leaving! Oh, no! Your wounds —"

"I'm well enough to travel, riding easy. It's best."

He tore his eyes from hers, his mouth hard-set, white around the lips. He stuck a thumb at Tomayo, who, smiling, hat in hand, bowed politely.

"We're doing no good here to anybody, the way things are. Folks think — well, they make it plain what they think of us. Nothing is ever going to change their minds about us. Being here, we're doing you no good. You most of all."

Marley, Scanlon, and Hamp moved closer within hearing, looking relieved and pleased. Gray raised his voice. "If you can spare a couple of horses and saddles —"

Making no bones over his eagnerness to see the last of them, Hamp said, "Sure, we can fix you up. We'll take yours in trade when I find who's holdin' 'em. Where you headed?"

"Denver," said Tomayo. "For my chest, you know." He coughed gently. "Then Salt Lake City. I plan to write a treatise on Mormon medical practices there, for my European colleagues."

The three men slowly digested the information. "That's a right long trip," observed Marley.

"We hope it is long enough to meet with your approval, gentlemen." Tomayo turned to Anne. "Dear lady, it is quite impossible to express in words our gratitude — our deep appreciation of all your kindness — our most sincere and heartfelt —"

She didn't hear, was not listening to him. She was gazing up into Gray's face, solemnly, earnestly. "You'll come back, won't you?"

He nodded.

"Promise?"

He almost retched in shame and self-disgust. "Yes, I'll come back . . ."

They rode northeast together over rolling range and piñon hills, as though short-cutting toward the river trail to Santa Rosa and on up straight north. At the last minute before their departure from Twin Peaks,

Marley and Scanlon had allowed awkwardly and uncomfortably that maybe it was all a mistake, their being taken for Blakeville badmen on the prowl. An ex-officer might turn his hand to a dirty dollar; a rebel at that. But not likely a doctor. No need to. Still, you couldn't be too careful.

They didn't precisely apologize, nor did they offer farewell handshakes. And Ira Hamp eyed grudgingly the two good Twin Peaks horses that Gray and Tomayo had picked for themselves. He muttered something about trading for pigs in a poke.

Gray rode looking straight ahead, his face stonily composed, his feelings in a battle. He had the strict conviction that he should be riding away forever from Twin Peaks. Opposing it was the wild wish to go back, and mocking that was the knowledge that he would . . . to loot the safe. It was the least of the evils to which he was committed. He tried to believe that it would add just one more regret to the pile, but he knew it wasn't so.

Tomayo, regarding Gray sidelong, said, "If Wallace is anything like his neighbors, the chances are good that he will come a cropper. I can't see such simpletons as Marley and Scanlon and their like outwitting His Honor and bringing him to his knees! These people are as thick-headed as their cattle. It will go hard on them when His Honor smashes them and takes over in the name of law and order! He will not forgive them."

He was meditative for a moment, then said in a changed tone, "When the smash comes, I shall do what I can to take care of the young lady."

It had the sound of a grave promise, rather than a taunt, but Gray countered harshly, "Maybe I'll be around to tend to that!"

Tomayo turned his face away, smiling faintly. "Maybe," he murmured.

At the crest of a high line of hills, they halted and carefully scanned the surrounding country. From that distance, the house and outbuildings of Twin Peaks were square specks and the broad yard was a small brown patch. They could see for miles over the range, grass-furred and rock-studded, with its bunches of cattle here and there slowly congregating at water holes as the heat of the day advanced.

Nobody was following them, spying on them to make sure that they kept a direct course out of the country. That was another indication that these Sierra Verde cowmen, for all their ready suspicion and belligerence, possessed the fault common to honest men: they lacked wary persistence. The virtue of vigilance, unending and unwearying vigilance, held its foremost place among rascals. Honest men tired of it, eased off the strain of constant precaution, and were apt to shift their reliance to a complacent faith that right made might.

Gray and Tomayo descended the north slope. They reined in, dismounted, and loosened cinches. While Gray stayed with the horses, Tomayo climbed on foot back up to the crest and flattened out behind a dwarf piñon to keep watch on Twin Peaks. The hot day dragged on, and he lay patiently, never asking Gray to relieve him. They had brought along no food. The water in their canteens had to be shared with the horses. Both animals, uneasy in strange hands and bothered by the long halt, stamped restlessly and kept their ears pointed in the direction of home.

In midafternoon, Tomayo called down to Gray, "About ten riders dropped in. Didn't stay long. Marley and Scanlon left soon afterward. Hamp left hours ago. No more callers today, I fancy, but we can't be sure." He rolled over onto his back and lighted a cigar. To Gray, below, he looked oddly like a small boy sneaking a forbidden smoke.

A cooling breeze sprang up after sundown. Darkness closed in, edged on the east by the pale spray of the rising moon. Gray tied the restless horses and went up the hill. A single light winked from Twin Peaks, and he and Tomayo lay watching it for a long time in silence.

Occupied with his own thoughts, Gray started slightly when Tomayo, without any preamble, asked him, "You grew up in Texas, didn't you?"

"Yes. Down on the Nueces, on a bit of a ranch. Born there. Why?"

"Was that where you knew" — Tomayo nodded toward the distant tiny light — "her?"

Gray frowned and gave no reply, and presently Tomayo murmured, "Wallace will be killed when His Honor takes over, you may be sure, and no mercy will be shown to his sister — his next of kin, supposedly. Better then for her *not* to be his sister! Is she, or is she not? It can do no harm to tell me."

"And what good would it do?" Gray demanded.

Tomayo plucked a stem of grass and chewed on it ruminatively. "You may happen to die, too, you know, before this is finished," he replied with calm practicality. "In that sad event, who will explain her position to His Honor? To whom would he listen?"

"You? Why would you?"

"Call it a whim. I have never won a woman's gratitude or respect. It would be a new experience. The Sierra Verde is going to be a tightly closed and ruled range, and hell will run amuck during the period of adjustment. I could prevail upon His Honor to give me permission, as one of my rewards for good service, to escort her safely out of it . . . perhaps to another country."

"As *your* sister?"

With a wave of his hand, Tomayo brushed off Gray's savage sarcasm. "Do not mistake my motives. Should you die, it would please me to do her that favor. Death is the final failure. By rescuing the lovely lady in distress, I would be pleased to prove that, of the two of us, I am the better man!"

Looking long at him, Gray could believe it. He wondered how often in his life the strange little man had been driven by the compulsion to prove himself better than other men, and what the proving had cost in treachery and bloodshed. The ordinary motives of men were not sufficient for Tomayo.

"All right," Gray said after lengthy consideration. "If that's how it is, I'll tell you what I know — and what I don't know . . ."

Tomayo waited patiently while Gray,

155

marshaling his thoughts, stared at the distant light of Twin Peaks. The thoughts brought pain to unhealed wounds, and Gray's voice was weighted with it when he spoke.

"Her name," he said, "was Anne Provost. The Provost ranch lay next to ours, on the Nueces, so you might say we grew up together. I was eighteen when Texas seceded, and naturally I enlisted in the Texas Brigade. Anne was sixteen. The day I was to go, a pony preacher came through. We got him to marry us — secretly. Her folks wouldn't have stood for it, 'specially her mother. My father had taken to drink and died broke. And me going right off to war."

"Was your marriage, ah, consummated?"

"No. We did it to — well, to bind us together, no matter what might happen." Gray paused, remembering that day. The whispered vows, the tears, the parting. "I never did get a furlough. Something always came up. Her father was killed the last year of the war. Wesley Provost. A good man. Some Indians shot him. At that time, Apaches were raiding along the border, taking advantage of the war and the fact that there weren't enough able men left at home to fight 'em off. They'd raid every night there was a moon, then scoot for Mexico

156

with all they could steal."

"The scoundrels!" commented Tomayo indulgently. "They remind me of my mother's tribe. Any cannibalism?"

"I reckon not, but they tortured anybody they —"

"Well, of course that goes without saying. My mother's tribe practiced various depraved forms of unpleasantness, I understand, before feasting." It was impossible to tell from Tomayo's smooth face whether or not he was speaking seriously.

"The next full moon after Wesley Provost was killed, the Apaches raided again. They wiped out the Provost ranch. They killed Mrs. Provost and threw her body in the burning house. They carried Anne off alive. I didn't know about it till months later, when the war was over and I got home."

Pensively, Tomayo tapped his thumbnail against his small white teeth. "Can't understand why they didn't eat her! Delectable!"

Gray glared at him for the grisly facetiousness. "I was told," he went on, "that a man rode on the trail of the Apaches and caught up with them. He was a captured Union spy, they said, who had escaped and was headed south for Mexico on a stolen horse. He was armed and desperate, and he'd shot a couple of fellers in his getaway. He jumped the Apaches, or they jumped him, or maybe he tricked them. Anyhow, it was known for sure that he managed to take Anne away from them."

"Quite a man!"

"Yeah. But then he bolted on to Mexico . . . and took her with him!"

"The spoils of war!"

"I went searching into Mexico, but months had gone by since he had disappeared with her, and Mexico was in a jumble with the revolt against Maximilian. I spent years following up cold trails, false leads, hints, a word here and there . . ." Gray shook his head slowly, his eyes sightless in far brooding. "The hunt took me all over Mexico. *Ranchos*. Army camps and *bandido* hangouts — anywhere I heard of a *norteamericano* who had a woman with him. Villages and towns and seaports. Gambling palaces and the lowest dives. Not a trace. I never learned whether she was dead or alive or what."

"Nor whether she went with that man willingly, eh?"

"She wouldn't have done that! Not Anne!"

Tomayo shrugged lightly. "None so blind — ! By the way, did she have a brother?"

"No. She was the Provosts' only child."

"And here you find her at last, posing as

158

Russell Wallace's sister! Mistress of Twin Peaks!" Tomayo snickered. "She has had an interesting career! Married to you, though in name only, then off to Mexico with an escaped Union spy, and now —"

"I didn't say she's Anne Provost," Gray cut in. "I just don't know. Anne was only sixteen when I last saw her. I've changed an awful lot since then." He absently ran his fingers over his scarred and unshaven face. "She could've changed, too. I can only remember her as she was then. Anne Wallace looks like her. But every time I see a woman with black hair and green eyes, I think for a minute she might be —"

"For a minute!" Tomayo echoed. "It is more than a minute this time, eh? Still, your memory could be at fault. You have carried an ideal image of her in your mind. The image could have become gradually altered, without your knowing it, each time you saw a woman who resembled her in some way. Then you meet Anne Wallace, and — presto, she is the ideal! Anne is not an uncommon name, either."

He spread his hands, palms upward. "However, that is pure supposition. Does it dispel the coincidence that she does resemble your Anne and bears the same first name? Does it explain away the fact that she is a Texan and her alleged brother is not?"

"No," Gray said heavily, "it doesn't."

"We may at least assume, then, for the sake of her future welfare, that she is not the sister of Russell Wallace!"

The tiny light winked out at last, leaving only the dark horizon and long streaks of moonlight on east-faced folds of range.

"Let us hie hence to the plunder!" murmured Tomayo, and they rose to their feet.

They descended the hill to their waiting horses, tightened the slackened cinches, and mounted. Not exchanging another word, they rode up over the hill and followed a steady course back to Twin Peaks.

12
ROBBERS' RETURN

The house and outbuildings of Twin Peaks loomed up, silent and unlighted, and Gray felt a totally unreasonable anger at the unguardedness of the place. Security in the Sierra Verde was of such long standing that its people were unaccustomed to strict caution. A woman could spend the night alone on a ranch and nothing was thought of it. Nobody ever harmed a woman. Nobody in the Sierra Verde.

Leading their horses, Gray and Tomayo skirted around to the corrals. On home ground, the two Twin Peaks horses walked confidently and none too quietly, looking forward to grain, and both registered snorting discontent when their reins were tied to a corral post. But anyone chancing to hear them would most likely attribute the sounds to some of the penned animals and not come out to investigate . . . or, at any rate, so Gray and Tomayo hoped, as they paced noiselessly up to the yard.

They knew their bearings, and entering into the shadows of the immense old cottonwoods, they went directly to the little ranch office. The door was locked, for a wonder; it was probably the only door not left unlocked night and day for fifty miles around, Gray guessed. He tried the window and found it fastened, too. Marley and Scanlon, or Ira Hamp, had seen to that much, at any rate.

Tomayo stepped to the window. By drawing himself up, he reached the middle sash. The slender blade of a knife flashed briefly in his hand, and there came a scraping sound and a faint click. He raised the window.

"All right, I am going in! Stand watch!"

"Go ahead, I'm right behind you. I can watch from inside just as well."

They slid through the opened window into the office. Here it was dark, and they didn't close the drape, a blanket. Gray lost sight of Tomayo, but he heard a metallic jingle from the vicinity of the safe. As his eyes became better adjusted, he saw it — a large safe, its top as high as his chin, the door massively hinged and steel-strapped.

He couldn't see what Tomayo was doing, except that he was on his knees, until he moved closer and peered down over his head. Tomayo was studiously making tests on the impressively big lock with what was evidently a handy little pocket kit of picklocks and skeleton keys.

In under five minutes, Bas Tomayo, master of devious crafts, whispered, "Gray, you owe me twenty dollars!"

He drew open the heavy door of the safe and went to ransacking inside, spilling out ledgers and papers onto the floor like a burrowing terrier.

"Here we are!" He backed out with a sizable tin cashbox, wrenching open its lid. "Ah — banknotes! Bundles of lovely, lovely banknotes! How considerate of them to make it so easy to carry!"

Gray said, "Here's your twenty," digging

it out of his pocket.

"Keep it! I have enough here!"

Possession of the money had wrought a change in Tomayo, the sight and feel of the packets of crisp banknotes lifting him to a state of exaltation. His former chilly aplomb gave way to a feverish glee. He fondled the money gloatingly, like a miser, or like a prisoner secretly cherishing his means of escape from hated bondage.

"Europe! Paris and Rome! Vienna! . . ."

Gray said, "Not so fast!" If there had to be a showdown, he would force it now and have done with it. He put a hand on the cashbox. "I'm in charge of this till we get back to Blakeville!"

Their faces were only inches apart in the shrouding darkness. "You?" Tomayo's giggle was as eerie as the stare of his yellow eyes. "You, *hombre?*"

"Let go of it!"

"You'll never live to see —" Tomayo began the worn phrase, and Gray stiffened in swift recognition of a rush of memory, recalling the revelation that had come to him for an instant during the getaway from Trail Fork.

Sounds somewhere outside in the quiet night jerked their heads up, nerves taut. The sounds, growing louder and clearer, resolved into the footsteps of several men hurrying through the ranch yard. There had been no previous noise of horses, and there was none now — only the trotting of men on foot.

While he listened, Gray stared in recollection into the blinding white flash he had had with his head wound, and he examined the flicker of thought that had come with it. The thought was a sinister one, but he guessed it was true. He guessed he knew why the Judge had sent Bas Tomayo after him.

Tomayo suddenly swung away from Gray, pulling the cashbox free from under Gray's hand and whispering thinly, as if to himself, "Time to go!" His right arm moved fast.

Gray hit him a shade faster than the draw. It was an uppercut to the chin and stretched Tomayo up straight on tiptoe, a look of sheer outrage in his eyes. The next one bowed him backward. Gray grabbed hold of him before he fell and laid him down on the floor without a thump.

The cashbox overturned among the spilled contents of the safe. Gray gathered up the packets of banknotes and stuffed them inside his shirt, then stood listening again to the hurried footsteps. The men had cut past the cottonwoods and seemed to be running to the house.

It was time to go, as Tomayo had said.

Tomayo, though, was not going anywhere for a while. He was out cold. He would know better than to rely entirely on a fast gun, next time, if the Sierra Verde crowd didn't hang him first. A good thing if they did, Gray told himself.

Yet he hesitated, scowling down at Tomayo, reluctant to leave the little man lying there to be caught red-handed amidst the stark evidence of robbery. He muttered, "I'm as guilty as he is. Worse, if —"

A door crashed, and the booted feet clattered on the floorboards of the front entrance to the house, becoming less loud as they trod on carpet. Some pieces of furniture, table or chair, blundered into, tumbled noisily, and a man swore at it. Gray drew his brows together, puzzled. It was surely out of the ordinary for Sierra Verde men to burst into the home of a neighbor, at night and without ceremony, and utter blackmouth within the hearing of a woman.

The voice of Anne Wallace called out from upstairs, "Who is it?" She sounded more surprised than alarmed. She, too, was accustomed to security and to the comfortable belief that no harm could befall a woman here.

There was a short silence before a man answered, "Friends o' Wallace. He home?"

"No, Russ is away. Who — ?"

"Who's here 'sides you?"

"Nobody. Who *are* you?"

"You better come down."

Another silence. A light wavered. "I don't know any of you men!"

"Don't get excited! When d'you look for Wallace back?"

"If I knew, I wouldn't tell it to strangers! I don't know you!"

"We could get acquainted while we wait for him! Come on downstairs!"

"How dare you — !"

"Come on down, princess — or I can come up!"

Anne Wallace said, "No!" then uttered a cry; Gray dived out through the open window of the ranch office.

Picking himself up from a headlong sprawl, Gray raced limpingly across the moonlit yard to the portico. The front door of the house yawned wide open; the downstairs hall, directly before him, contained six men. A seventh man was slowly mounting the stairs toward Anne, who, dressed in a white robe, held a lighted lamp above her head as if prepared to throw it.

The men were ragged, dirty, heavily armed. Three of them carried rifles in addition to their belted guns and sheath knives.

They all had the earth-grained and hairy appearance of having recently emerged from long skulking in some hidden boar's den of a camp. They had not shed their brush manners. The air smelled of whiskey and stale sweat.

The man on the stairs wore a blue bandanna tied over his head in lieu of a hat, its loose ends dangling stringily down the back of his short neck. He was thickset, of powerful physique, and held his arms apart from his body like a wrestler in the ring.

Foresight played no part whatever in Gray's reaction to the sight of Anne at bay before these hard-bitten invaders. Rage flooded out the impersonal calmness that was the foundation of his gun training, and stepping into the open doorway he said in a voice not his own, "Hold it, you scum — hold it right there!"

The six men in the hall whirled immediately to face him, disregarding his command. A lawless existence in mountain caves and thickets had sharpened them to an animal-like wildness. They stared at Gray, not cowed by his drawn guns but instantly alert. Because of his bandaged head, he wore his hat tipped forward. The light from Anne's lamp at the top of the staircase reached only the lower line of his jaw.

The man on the stairs turned half around, more slowly than the others, showing a matted black beard and a barrel chest. Getting a clear view of him, Gray harked back to what the Judge had told him before he set out from Blakeville: there was a man named Froke, head of a gang of stock thieves operating from up near the Sangres, who had tried to earn the bounty offered for Russell Wallace's capture, and who, to keep the field clear for himself, may have betrayed others who had tried.

"Froke!" he said. "If that's who you are, scat off back to your hole and take your scum with you!"

"That's me, all right, Ned Froke!" The brush-jumper's bloodshot eyes rested appraisingly on Gray's guns. The guns were worn smooth from use, and each had a front inch of trigger guard cut away. Froke twitched a thick eyebrow.

He had been a notorious hotshot, according to the Judge, until drink blunted his judgment, and then a bad bobble or two had dulled his trust in his own speed. His chronic fault was that he couldn't see very far ahead. Neither whiskey nor wounds had impaired his bull nerve, though. He could still coolly size up an unexpected situation.

He asked Gray thoughtfully, "Now who in hell would you be?"

"You heard what I said! I'd as soon shoot as say it again!" The flat menace in Gray's tone caused the three men bearing rifles to still their sly moves to put him in muzzle-point. "The lady wants you gone!"

With heavy playfulness, Froke reached upward to take Anne's hand. "Aw, she ain't said so, have you, princess? I say from here, now, you're —"

Gray fired. He shot at Froke's reaching arm and an instant later slapped an uplifted rifle with a bullet that wrecked the breech and the fingers of the man holding it.

Anne shook, startled. The flame of the lamp in her raised hand glittered and smoked. She showed fear now, as she looked at Gray down at the far end of the hall. Gray's eyes glimmered, deadly violent, malevolent.

Froke pushed back his shirtsleeve and studied his blood-streaked forearm. He heaved his massive shoulders forward, then slowly relaxed. Eying Gray, he said, "You're a leetle quick on the shoot! I oughta know who you are, but blast me if I can place you. You called me by name."

The flickering of the unsteady lamp took

his notice, and he swung his bandanna-clad head around to look up at it. Anne, in an instinctive gesture of defense, raised the lamp higher, as if to throw it.

Flinching, Froke exclaimed, "Don't you chuck that at me! Holy Moses!" His hairy head and beard rendered him all too vulnerable to fire. He betrayed more uneasiness over that than he did over Gray's guns.

"All right, bad *hombre!*" He moved down a step, warily watching the lamp but speaking to Gray. "Pull your hackles down, we're goin'." Then, to his men: "Take a good peek at him, boys, will you? I sure do want to know who he is."

Gray put his back to the wall and let them file past. Each man stared in turn at him, trying to discern his features beneath the hat brim. He thought he recognized a couple of them from some casual encounter in the past, probably in Mexico. The rest were unknown to him.

Ned Froke, last one to leave, gave Gray a nod that revealed no especial enmity. "Here on, y'know, I'll have to keep an eye out for you," he promised. "A big larrikin with a limp, a bandage on his noggin, an' a funny way of pointin' his irons — only you won't point 'em at me again if I see you first. 'Night, princess!" he called back to Anne and lumbered on out, casually shaking a trickle of blood from his hand.

Gray followed him a pace to the door, motioning up at Anne to shield the lamp so that its light wouldn't outline him. He heard the men troop off. They walked unhurriedly, knowing that the ranch hands were out on roundup. Froke mumbled a few words, and they hastened a trifle. The sounds of their footsteps faded as they tramped on to wherever they had left their horses, and the ranch fell quiet once more.

Gray became aware of Anne descending the stairs with the lamp. In the hall, she sent him a questioning look, and he nodded and said, "They're gone."

She did not speak of what he had just done, or ask him how he came to be at Twin Peaks when supposedly he and Tomayo were heading up north to Denver. She glided swiftly by him, the hem of her robe skimming the floor. He watched her leave the house; watched her carry the lamp through the front portico, her slippered feet flying soundlessly over the flagstones; watched, impotent, as she turned left toward the ranch office under the cottonwoods. The war chest of the Sierra Verde Pool — the all-important money, earmarked for Russell

Wallace's use — was her most urgent concern.

He wanted to run to his waiting horse and ride away, but he couldn't force himself to do it. He followed her unwillingly, dreading what he knew she must find.

13

CAPTAIN GALAHAD

Anne unlocked the door of the ranch office and, holding the lighted lamp before her, passed on inside. Her cry of dismay cut Gray like the whimper of a hurt child. He entered in behind her and saw all that she saw — the gaping door of the big old safe, the spilled ledgers and papers, the looted cashbox. The brutal disorder left by plunderers in the night.

Bas Tomayo, on the floor, showed every sign of having been a victim rather than a perpetrator of the robbery. Propped on one elbow, he was dabbing at his bruised and cut chin and gazing vacantly at the traces of blood that it left on his hand. The coming of light into the room hastened the rise of his senses. Into his yellow eyes crept a glint of bitter rancor. He stopped shaking his head and ran a baleful stare up Gray from feet to face. Gray kept a gun out and met Tomayo's look stonily.

"The money! It's gone!" Anne spun around to Gray. The rush of air flared the lamp. Her words came in a stammer of despair. "Gone! The safe — look — !"

He said nothing. His deep-set eyes, trained to an opaque blankness in emergency, met her stricken look. Here was his test. He had to go through with this without taking a single weak or hesitant step. Conscience would not survive this deed, and success meant freedom at last from its futile nagging. Failure meant downfall, the inevitable coming of the catastrophe that overtook men of his kind when they gave way to indecision.

He only thought his eyes were blank.

Strange and warring expressions crossed Anne's paled face: incredulousness; shrinking doubt; a heartbreaking edge of suspicion.

"The — the window. It was forced open. It must have been done very quietly, or — or I would have heard from my bedroom."

She spoke haltingly, as if ashamed of what she was saying and of what she was going to say.

"And — and this safe was opened quietly, too. Opened at the lock. It's not damaged.

It wasn't broken open. The lock was — picked."

She turned the lamp up brighter, fumbling with it.

"That man," she stammered on. "You — you called him Froke. M-my brother has had some trouble with the Froke gang, but they never dared to come right onto our place before tonight. They weren't very quiet. I heard them coming through the yard. They — they didn't seem to stop by here. I don't think they knew about the safe. Even if they did, I d-don't think they could have opened it like this. They're stock thieves and holdup men. Not — not expert lock pickers!"

She gazed down at Tomayo on the littered floor and asked him pleadingly, "How is it that you are here, Doctor? Was it you who forced open the window? Surely you didn't come back to — to rob us, did you?"

Tomayo, whose eyes had been fixed unwaveringly on her since her first word, moved his head slightly in negation that carried more conviction than a hundred vehement denials.

She drew a deep breath before putting her next question to him. "Who stole the money?"

He straightened a forefinger at Gray and

didn't speak.

Like someone in the unnatural composure of sleepwalking, Anne faced Gray. "Were you in here earlier tonight? Was it actually from here that you came over to the house?"

Gray, his mouth dry and tasting of ferrous metal, could find nothing to say to her.

Her shoulders drooped. She set the lamp down on the desk wearily, as if lacking strength to hold it any longer. Huskily, she said, "Yes. I know you did. I see it in your eyes. A lie wouldn't help, would it? Not now. *You* stole the money! *You!*"

Her somber apathy dissolved suddenly under a storm of emotion. Wrath flamed in her eyes. Her forlornly drooping body came erect and taut, the rich mass of hair tossing back, the faint blue veins throbbing in her white throat.

"Thief!"

She was a blazingly angry young woman, condemning furiously an idol whose crumbling clay had destroyed her faith and sacrificed her pride on a false altar.

"Thief! Hypocrite!"

Her voice did not go shrill and frenzied, nor loud. It scarcely rose above a whisper, yet it was penetrating, as audible as the hiss and crack of a whiplash.

"They warned me against you! I wouldn't

listen to them. I vouched for your honesty. Your honesty! They were right about you, and I was wrong — wrong — wrong! Thief and traitor!"

She stood like a wild tigress, panting with fury, clawing him with every recrimination at her command.

"You promised to come back, didn't you? And you did come back — oh, you did! In the night! To rob the house that gave you shelter — that gave you help when you badly needed it! You unprincipled black-guard!" she denounced him passionately. "The lowest pickpocket would have more honor!"

Sitting up, Tomayo wagged his head in sad disapproval at Gray and sighed, "Corrupted by evil companions in his youth, no doubt!" He glanced into the cashbox, saw that it was empty, and his disapproval became more acute.

Gray's face was bloodless and drawn, distorted by muscles bunched over clenched jaws. Gone was the opaque stare.

Anne made to speak again. He had to stop her. His endurance had reached its limit. He glowered down at her and commanded harshly, "Shut up!"

She met his eyes squarely. "Not while you are here! If you don't like to hear the truth about yourself — go! I can't prevent you from running off with your loot, can I? Go, you lying, cheating, thieving —"

"Shut up!" he thundered, and now his eyes were nearly crazed.

She thought he was about to strike her down, for he drew back his arm, doubling it at the elbow as if to deliver a driving punch. She flinched, then stood ready to receive the expected blow. But instead he ripped open his shirt from neck to waist. He thrust wads of banknotes at her, tumbling them out from under his shirt as though they were hot coals burning him, letting them fall anywhere before she could take them.

Bas Tomayo let out a moan of anguish at seeing a fortune treated so disrespectfully. He scuttled forward over the floor, his hands outstretched to gather up the precious harvest.

Gray, savagely glad to vent his feelings on somebody, stuck the gun at him and snarled, "Back off! You ever touch that money again, I'll blast you down! It goes back where it belongs!"

One look at Gray's face, and Tomayo backed off, worry in his eyes. "You madman!" he muttered. "Judas! Sir Galahad spurns the Grail?"

Gray drove him at gunpoint into a corner,

not trusting him an inch. Over his shoulder he told Anne, "Pick up the money and get back to the house!" To Tomayo he said, "Turn around and face the wall. Don't make any mistake — this gun's ready to go off!"

"I believe you," Tomayo admitted and obeyed.

Gray plucked Tomayo's guns from him. He pitched them out through the window and said, "When you find 'em, keep on going and don't come back! It's high time we parted company for good. Right?"

"Time parts the best of friends," Tomayo concurred. "So does money, come to think of it. I bid you farewell — for now."

"S'long."

Leaving him standing there like a naughty schoolboy in the corner, Gray walked out. Beyond the shading cottonwoods, a white-robed figure waited, hair glossy in the moonlight. The tempest in him had subsided, but he snapped roughly:

"Get into the house, I said! Hide that money —"

"Wait!" she broke in. Her eyes shone wet. "P-please don't tell me to shut up, b-because I won't! Oh, I'm so horribly ashamed! I should have known!"

He walked toward her. "Known what?

That I'm everything you called me, and more?"

Her attempt to smile at him was a tremulous failure. "Of course not. Don't say that. It's all so clear to me now, I can't imagine how I ever. . . . It was he who robbed the safe — Dr. Maroon, if he really is a doctor. You followed him and caught him at it. You knocked him out and took the money away from him. But because he had been your friend, you wouldn't denounce him, even when I . . ."

She hid her face from him, burying it in the packets of banknotes that she carried in both hands against her chest.

"You saved us all tonight. Russ — me — everybody in the Sierra Verde. This money means so much to all of us. And I called you a thief and a traitor!"

A gunshot cracked from somewhere in the direction of the corrals, and a bullet pinged past between them. On the instant, Gray jumped at Anne and pulled her down to the ground with him. His first thought was of Tomayo. But there hadn't been time enough for Tomayo to retrieve his guns and slip off to try a bushwhack.

"Get into the house," Gray said to Anne, releasing her, "while I tend to that joker!"

He drew his guns and called out on

179

speculation, "Froke, you're a lousy shot by moonlight! I'm coming to show you how! Stay right there!" He rocked up onto his feet and advanced at a weaving run, spacing shots at the spot where the gun-flash had appeared.

His guess fell right. Ned Froke bellowed an oath of disgust and took off, heard but not seen. Shooting by moonlight was tricky at best, and when luck didn't ride his bullet, a sensible man quit.

Gray turned back. Looking into the office, he saw that Tomayo had departed, and he went on into the main house. Lamps were lighted in the front room downstairs. There he found Anne. She had piled the money on a table.

There was an awkward silence between them, until Gray said, "I guess we could put that back in the safe now. My slick little partner has pulled out. So has Froke. I better stay by it the rest of the night, though."

"I — I think you had better."

They carried the money back, and he helped her tidy up the office. When all was in place again, she locked the safe. Gray closed and fastened the window and drew the blanket drape over it. A scrap of paper fell from an opened fold of the blanket. He picked it up. It was a scribbled note, and he read:

Captain Galahad —
The lady wins. You lost your trusty helper, your back-watcher. My loss is monetary. I hope to recoup. Keep your shirt on.

T.

Crumpling the note before Anne could see it, Gray grinned faintly over Tomayo's choice of words. There were few traits that could be counted to the credit of that little sinner, but one of them was an acid sense of humor. The veiled threat — *I hope to recoup* — was not to be taken lightly, however, and he told Anne, "I'll sit out the night here."

"I'll make you some coffee," she said, smiling, and Gray recalled his excuse to Marley and Scanlon when they had discovered him outside the office door. He guessed nothing would shake Anne's belief that he liked a nightly pot of coffee. Her every look and action manifested her frank wish to please him and to make up for what she thought had been a monstrous mistake on her part.

He would leave Twin Peaks, he promised

himself, as soon as it became safe for her.

Anne brought hot coffee and sandwiches from the house. She had snatched time to dress while there, abandoning all thought of retiring for the remainder of the night. "I'm much too wrought up to be able to sleep," she confessed.

Gray nodded. So was he, even had he contemplated sleeping. Unthinkingly, he asked her, "I don't suppose you've ever had to go through a night like this before, have you?" Only after he asked the question did he recognize the impulse behind it.

Setting out the coffee and sandwiches on the desk, she answered, "Not since I came here. This is a peaceful country, on the whole, or was until recently. But when I was younger — near the end of the war — things happened. . . ." She stopped.

Her back was partly toward him. He saw her shiver and heard her sigh. The black imps raged abruptly within him. He said to her, "So you haven't always lived here."

"No, Russ brought me here. My brother." She added nothing to the bare statement.

He could not, to save his life, have refrained from asking her one final question: "Have you ever been married?"

She stood quite still for a minute. Then she turned a flushed face to him and said in a low voice, "Yes. I was married at sixteen . . . to a boy who went off to the war. I haven't seen him since the day of our marriage. It was before the — the things happened."

Gray thought of the time in his own life when things had begun happening, bad things, and he wished with a fierce and impotent intensity that those things could have been far different for them both.

"I've heard that he came home when the war ended," Anne went on. "Then he disappeared. I loved him, yet — it's strange, I can hardly remember his face now." Her eyes took on a faraway, seeking look. She shook her head. "I can't *see* him anymore! Do you suppose that could mean he is dead?"

"Yes," Gray said. "That's what it means."

She said, "Whenever I have thought he might be dead, it always crushed me. I didn't want to live, if he was never coming back into my life. But now" — she shook her head again, wonderingly — "now I can't even feel very sad! I must be horribly hardhearted! Poor Alan! I hope he didn't waste too much time looking for me."

She was wearing a full-skirted dress, small at the waist, and over it she had slipped on a light woolen jacket against the night's coolness. From a loose pocket of the jacket she took out the key to the safe.

"Please keep this for me, will you?" she asked Gray. "Men have such better pockets."

With his eyes on her face, Gray slowly extended his hand to receive the key. This, he knew, was not purposely a gracious means of expressing her complete trust in him. Rather, it was simply a normal action, quite guileless and unconsidered . . . and the more sincere because of it.

And because he wasn't paying any attention to the key, his eyes being on her face, it slipped through his fingers when she passed it to him. They both stooped to pick it up from the floor between them, and her hair and his nose met.

Her hair was soft and his nose was hard, so neither came to harm, but their composure collapsed. Anne raised her head, laughing over the small accident. Gray looked full into her eyes, so close to his own that he could see the pupils expanding under his gaze. She ceased laughing, but her lips stayed parted.

His ruling thought was: *Whatever she has done — whatever she may have become — I can't go on without her.*

He put out his hands to her. She had not done up her hair when she dressed, except

184

to gather it back loosely with a comb or two and his hands plunged through the rich black tresses and met around her neck. A fallen comb danced on the floor. He drew her up close and found that her eyes were suddenly brimming with tears. Her hands touched him. Her lips moved readily to meet his, and he was aware of soft pressure filling his arms. The coffee cooled in the cups.

14
MASTER OF TWIN PEAKS

Gray picked up the key to the safe. His hand shook; he noted it and realized that he was trembling from head to foot. A pitiless clarity of mind then forced upon him the perception of his position; its entrapment stood complete, its mire of secrecy and guilt was impossible to cleanse.

He said hoarsely, more to himself than to Anne, "There must be some way to work things out! There's got to be! God, if only we could change everything!"

Shining-eyed, radiant, Anne answered him warmly, "But we can! We can cast off what mistakes we've made and start a fresh life! And how wonderful — how gloriously wonderful it's going to be!"

She gave a happy little laugh. Her soaring optimism was not to be bounded by any material trammels. No obstacles existed for her that she could not overcome.

"Already, I'm a different person to what I was before" — her color rushed high — "to what I used to be. I was lonely. Unhappy. I suppose that's the real reason I kept Alan in my memory. He's gone now."

"Russ — ?" Gray spoke the name with difficulty.

"Russ never met him," she said. Then, with a kind of gentle diffidence, "You remind me of Alan, a little. His eyes were the same color as yours, and his hair. And he always wanted to change everything for the better . . . always wishing for a miracle."

"Miracles don't happen," Gray responded automatically. "I found that out."

Her eyes reflected the hurt puzzlement of a woman in love whose man carelessly lets drop a cynical blasphemy in the hallowed halls of her adoration. Softly, she said, "Isn't this a miracle that we have? It is to me. And we shall have more. Is there something wrong? You look — strange."

"No," Gray said. His voice sounded dead and hollow in his own ears. His face felt stiff, eyes smarting dry as though from alkali dust, bitterness filling his mouth. "No, nothing's wrong. There isn't going to be." She smiled again, not knowing that his meaning was that he was going to leave her. The scales stood too far out of balance; there was too much guilt on his side, too little on hers. There were worse burdens to bear than loneliness, even for a woman, he believed; even for her, a woman who was made to love and to be loved.

It was while they paused, occupied with widely different thoughts of the future, that Gray heard a steady trot of horses beating a muffled tattoo. He listened intently, dropping his hands to his holstered guns. Two horses, carrying riders. They came clopping onto the hard surface of the ranch yard.

A man's whistle shrilled a single rising note, and Anne flew to the door and flung it open. She gave back the whistle like a boy, in exact imitation.

"Russ!" she called, running out into the yard. "Russ! Welcome home!"

Russell Wallace turned out to be tall and thin and razor-edge straight. In appearance and manner, he gave the impression of being almost old enough to be Anne's father. It required closer study to perceive that he was in fact considerably younger than he seemed to be at first sight. He displayed the curt forcefulness and authority of a veteran campaigner, and Gray could well understand why this man was the chosen leader, the head and driving spirit of the Sierra Verde Pool.

As soon as he stamped into the ranch office, he leveled a penetrating stare at Gray and rasped down deep in his throat, "Gr-rr-*hup!*"

What that signified could have been anything. Gray thought it resembled the bristling growl of a Northern patrol commander who sighted a Confederate outpost in reportedly Union country. His neck hairs prickled with instant hostility.

Russell Wallace had a hatchet face, barbed with a beak nose that jutted above dangling cavalry mustaches as long and as pointed as daggers. The mustaches added years to his looks, but in addition he was the kind of man who at twenty could probably have passed for forty; and when he reached forty, he would be regarded as old by men older than himself.

Except for the powdering of dust, his severely neat clothes — town suit of dark broadcloth, plain black boots, low-crowned hat — might have been fitted on him by a valet, or more likely a meticulous army orderly, fifteen minutes ago. He even wore gloves, bleached buckskin gloves which he removed with somewhat finical deliberateness, tugging them loose a finger at a time, meanwhile keeping his piercing eyes fixed on Gray.

Trading him stare for stare, Gray could not help feeling uncomfortably grubby by contrast. His unshaven face with its accumulation of scars and dents; the soiled bandage around his head; his hard-worn and bloodstained garb; the low hang of his thonged holsters; everything about him added up to a ruffianly toughness. Becoming acutely conscious of the fact that he was also an intruder and an impostor, he reacted aggressively, hooking his thumbs over his gun belts and putting an arrogant tilt to his head.

Gravely, Wallace bent and kissed Anne on the cheek. His affection for her was evidently stored safely apart from contact with his personal dignity, and was to be demonstrated only when he let down his stiff reserve, if he ever did. Or perhaps the stranger's presence constrained him.

"What's been going on here?" he inquired crisply. "I met Hamp coming in. He's putting up my horse. Said he thought he heard gunfire a while ago."

"There was," Anne said. "The Froke gang

came here tonight and —"

"Good God! And you here alone! Who is this — hah — gentleman?"

"Captain Steel. He —"

"Hah! How d'you do, sir!"

The military title thawed the edges of Wallace's frigid austerity. He shook hands firmly with Gray. He accorded him a fraternal deference, as one ex-officer to another. He scanned him with searching approval, apparently seeking to ascertain from his looks and bearing what arm of service he had graced for the Union. Then he came out with it:

"What regiment, sir?"

"Texas Brigade, sir!"

"Oh. . . ."

Anne said, "The safe was robbed, too." Knowing Wallace's habit of interrupting, she forestalled him swiftly. "There are other things to tell, but they can wait. Captain Steel drove off the Froke gang and saved the money. If it had not been for him —"

"My deepest thanks, sir!"

Russell Wallace shook hands with Gray once more. Gray guessed dourly that the matter of the Texas Brigade might even be overlooked, given much more of this kind of thing.

"Hamp" — Anne tapped Wallace on his

straight and well-clad shoulder — "Hamp has been telling you his side, I suppose, about Captain Steel, hasn't he, Russ?" Tactfully, she omitted mention of a certain Dr. Maroon. "The truth is, he was senselessly attacked in Trail Fork by Marley and Scanlon and several more of our friends! He was wounded! Hunted like an outlaw! He —"

Wallace's snort shook his fierce mustaches. "Hamp's a fool! He never should have left you here alone on the place! The work doesn't mean that much to me, not by a long shot, Anne! Marley's another fool, and some of the rest aren't much better. Business and profits, and defend themselves in their spare time — by shooting the first stranger who happens to come their way!"

"He was unconscious when he came here," Anne inserted.

Wallace didn't inquire into Gray's method of finding his way there in that condition. And he showed a singularly obtuse streak by failing to detect the tone of Anne's voice when she spoke of Gray and the look in her eyes.

"They can't get it through their thick heads that they won't have any business and profits to worry about if Judge Blake takes over the Sierra Verde!" he declared. "Gr-rr-hup! It's like counting the cost of powder when you're under attack. Eh, Captain? When your life is at stake —"

"Captain Steel risked his life tonight," Anne quietly reminded him. "He risked it for me and for our money. I'm sure he didn't count the cost."

Wallace then shot a long look at her and dropped his irascible heedlessness. "No higher recommendation is possible to me than Anne's praise," he assured Gray. "Aside from the money, your service to her places me in your debt. I hope you'll stay on with us. If a fight interests you — and I fancy it does — we have a thundering good one coming up!"

His stilted manner was not a pose, Gray realized, nor was his tendency toward florid speech an affectation. Whether or not he saw himself as a peppery old soldier — at thirty-five or thereabouts — the part came natural to him, and he fitted into it. He must have picked it up in the Army, where it became fastened onto him like an ineradicable tic; some men simply never recovered from officer rank. But at any rate he wasn't faking it.

"Thanks, but I won't be here long," Gray replied, and Anne gazed at him uncomprehendingly.

Russell Wallace paid Anne a further musing regard. He thumbed his mustaches, frowning. He made a minor ceremony of producing two slim black cheroots, handed one of them to Gray as though bestowing a token of brotherhood, and struck a match for them both.

"I'm morally bound to induce you to stay," he vowed. "This is good cow country, and I take it you're a cowman born and bred. Unless you have better prospects in view elsewhere, or a private business that requires your own personal care and attention" — he ran a doubting glance over Gray's attire — "there's no reason for you to leave. No reason on earth, sir!"

"I've got to —" Gray began, but Wallace overrode him.

"Compared to your droughty Texas, this is a paradise! With all due respect to you — and to Anne, who knows my opinion — I do not have a high regard for Texas. I've been there. It was during the war, so conditions were unusual, it's true, but — never again! I left in a hurry, without regrets."

Gray froze inside as Wallace unwittingly revealed the picture: an unnamed Union spy, a desperate escapee who had shot a couple of men. . . . Yes, conditions were unusual. Saved a girl from Indian raiders, in his flight to Mexico. Took her along.

Vanished with her — but not deep down into the Mexican interior, no. He had not resorted to the course of a fugitive who, with an unwilling girl in tow, dared not return to his own country.

No; he had cut westward below the border with her and then crossed back north, into the Territory. He had brought her here to Twin Peaks, his home, and passed her off as his sister. He could not have managed that if she had refused. She must have come here willingly with him, and willingly stayed.

Wallace was saying, "Never again, I said, but the fact is that I've just come from the Panhandle. I didn't go far over the line, though." Catching Gray's expression and evidently thinking it reflected resentment at the slurs on Texas, he touched back to his former subject. "Only thing wrong with the Territory here is the politically rotten part of it — the part that's under Judge Blake's foot. You've heard of that cursed scoundrel, of course, and his Blakeville hell-hole."

He sighted his cheroot at Gray. "Take my word for it, we'll clean out him and his pack of thugs! He's more than just a rotten apple in the barrel. He's devilishly clever, and he knows the game. I don't underrate him — too many fools have, and they've paid hard for it! Greed? Why, the scoundrel is insatiable! He's got to be stopped, and we'll do it! A man owes it to his conscience, if nothing else. Let him go on, and the day will come when he'll be too big for anybody to stop."

He inhaled strong smoke, expelled it in a gust, and continued: "I got in touch with some of the people back in Washington. Asked for an official investigation of Judge Blake. Gave them facts. If he's allowed his way, I told them, he'll end up controlling the whole Territory. Hah! What good did it do? They all told me to see somebody else about it. Fools!"

There appeared to exist in this world a prevalence of fools, in his opinion. He said, "The only recourse for us is to take the law into our own hands. It's against my principles, but this involves the larger principle of fight or die. I've raised a company of vigilantes, all picked men, many of them Texans like yourself. My preparations are almost complete. Will you join us? Surely a fighter like you can't stand aside when the trumpet sounds!"

The grandiloquence did not move Gray. He was thinking of his long search throughout Mexico. The despair and black depression, the nightmare visions, and at last the abandoning of the search. The stupid, fruitless years. While Anne Provost — Anne Gray, his bride — lived quietly under the name of Anne Wallace, as the sister of Russell Wallace, up here in this north-central section of the New Mexico Territory.

And this man, the highly reputable master of Twin Peaks, the blackhearted jackleg he had hunted to kill, was urging him to stay and fight on his side. The outrageous irony of it all was a goad, but angry laughter was far from him. He felt stale and empty and bitterly cheated.

"Good men," Wallace talked on, "are needed here. Not common gunmen. I'll have no truck with such trash! Men who, like you and me . . ."

15
ATTACK

Outside the office, Ira Hamp, coming up from tending to Wallace's horse, voiced a gruff, "Hey!" that carried a ring of querulous surprise.

Russell Wallace, breaking off his listing of good men's qualifications, frowningly pointed his beak nose at the open door. "It's all right, Hamp! Captain Steel is a friend!"

"Yeah? But what's — ?"

A chilling giggle cut across the foreman's grumbling question, and a gun spat one solid report. Unsteady footsteps scraped gravel. The giggle rippled forth, rising lightly to a pleased laugh.

Hamp lumbered into the lamplight at a staggering run. Dragging his feet, he hung a toe on the doorstep and pitched headlong into the office.

"The Mex!" he gasped. He rolled laboriously over onto his back, trying to struggle up. "Goddam little — ! He shot me! Laughed — an' shot me! Laughed!" It was like him to condemn the laugh along with the shot.

Wallace bent over to help him, and Hamp angrily flailed an arm at him. The front and back of Hamp's shirt hung wetly dark. He had been shot high in the middle of his back at close range, and the bullet had smashed on through his chest.

"Damn — your damn fight — Wallace! It don't — concern me! The damn work —"

He choked up and fell back, and his head bumped the floor. He would never get the work finished. Nor had he thought to give warning of the presence of Ned Froke and his men on the place, if he had seen them. A moment elapsed before they opened fire with a volley that brought echoes rattling back from the hills; and then Bas Tomayo could be heard cautioning them to let up on the racket.

Wallace hauled out a long Dragoon .44 from under his coat, took a fresh bite on his cheroot, and cast a glance of professional disparagement around the office. As a fort, it wasn't much. He kicked the door shut and bushed an eyebrow at Gray.

"Gr-rr-*hup!* Bad situation, Captain!"

"It is," Gray said. He meant, as did Wallace, that it could hardly be worse. By luck or design, the marauders had crept back and struck at precisely the right time for them. No; not luck, Tomayo being with them. Tomayo never trusted to luck. Design, then; Tomayo's design.

"The Froke gang, Captain, you think?"

"And another man with them. A little guy who's worse than the lot of 'em put together. A pint of poison! Watch out for that window!"

The window crashed in, behind its draped blanket, and Gray and Wallace fired together. Readying for the assault, they overturned the desk onto its side for Anne to crouch behind. It provided weak shelter, but might at least protect her from stray bullets. Gray cursed himself for being caught off guard, for allowing the trap to close in on them, and the thought recurred to him once more that he was slipping. He had given time to brooding, as neglectful of vigilance as Russell Wallace, while Tomayo seized advantage of that fatal error. Tomayo obviously had an understanding with Ned Froke, based on previous acquaintance, for they were calling each other by their first names.

A gun roared five times through the door, punching the lock into a twisted mass and sending splinters and bits of metal flying across the office. Two bullets tore chunks from the edge of the overturned desk. Gray, reaching for the lamp to blow it out, changed his mind as he heard Tomayo utter a sneering comment:

"Much good that does, Ned! I can't quite see you charging into the light! And don't depend on anyone else to do it — certainly not me!"

"We got to get Wallace, ain't we?" rumbled Froke. "He's in there!"

"Yes, and I know who else is in there!"

"Damn you, Bas, are you tryin' to rattle me? Quit it! Quit stallin'! Always got some cussed trick up your sleeve!"

"And my tricks usually work, which is more than can be said of yours lately," Tomayo chided him. "Now stop the shooting — all of you!"

"The hell —!" A rock hit the door a shattering blow. "We got to do it fast! Got to get out o' here before somebody hears us an' brings the whole —"

"Stop shooting!" — Tomayo's voice thinned almost to a scream — "His Honor wants Wallace alive, not dead! Alive on delivery, you fools, or no pay! No pay, understand?"

The sporadic gunfire ceased, and in the comparative hush following it, Froke argued, "So how about if we can just wing him? Put him out of action —"

"A devil of a job we would have, packing him down to Blakeville and explaining to His Honor!" Tomayo cut in. "I know what His Honor wants better than you do. Wallace is to be brought in quietly. It is to be made to appear that he might have come in of his own accord, bringing the war chest with him. His Honor would scalp you for shooting up the place and leaving signs of a fight! He does not like to see his plans go down the drain, Ned!"

"You shot first! You gunned down the —"

"You are mistaken! Hamp probably happened to discover Wallace preparing to abscond with the war chest to Blakeville, and Wallace killed the poor fellow! You had better pray that you have not hit the young lady — that's something we could not cover up! You would be on His Honor's blacklist!"

Gray glanced at Russell Wallace to see how he was taking it. Wallace's hatchet face was tightly frowning with the concentration of listening to the cold-blooded debate going on outside, and Gray guessed that he, too, was stabbed by a grim foreboding of what was coming. In arguing Froke out of shooting, Tomayo was only clearing the ground for deadlier tactics. To the little man's fertile brain, the solution to the stalemate was as simple as the sum of two and two.

Relinquishing the argument, Froke growled, "All right, smart boy, what do we do?"

"Find some coal oil. There must be some around, for the lamps." Tomayo spoke clearly. "We must cover up the signs of a fight here. Destroy the evidence, rather. A fire will do it nicely."

"Make a hell of a bonfire if these trees catch! Be seen for miles! Everybody'll come on the jump!"

"We'll be gone by then. We'll be on the go, while they are on the come! All right, now. A pail or two of coal oil . . . and gather some kindling while you are at it. Ned, would you stay in a burning building?"

201

"Am I crazy?"

Tomayo laughed. "A moot question. It does not apply to the occupants of this little edifice. As sensible people, they will remove themselves from the coming conflagration. I am not at all sure of the fireproof quality of that safe, so they should bring the money out with them." He paused and asked politely, "Am I heard and understood by all parties concerned?"

There was no misunderstanding him. His meaning was lucid, his reasoning perfectly logical. A tenacity of purpose ruled out any possibility that he might be bluffing. He would go through with it.

Gray, guns in his hands, ran a bleak look from the broken door to Russell Wallace. The two of them could make a break, lunge out shooting. . . .

As if the thought had reached him, Tomayo said, "There are eight of us! We have the door and the window covered!" A can clanked, and he murmured something to the man who brought it. Then he spoke again:

"We are going to burn this little building, whether you are in it or not! It will go up like a torch when we throw on the oil, you know, so you had better not wait! Won't you join us? Quietly, of course — there are some nervous triggers among us tonight!"

Froke's heavy voice broke in impatiently, "Cut the cackle an' let's roast 'em out! Gimme that oil!"

"Wait, Ned!"

"I waited months for this, an' I don't wait no more!"

Gray looked last at Anne. He took his eyes off her and said to Russell Wallace, "Drop your gun!"

Wallace reared back his head like a startled hawk.

"What? . . . " He saw Gray's guns veering to bear on him. He raised his eyes to the somber face above them. "Captain Steel — !"

Gray slapped out with a gun barrel. He knocked the Dragoon .44 from Wallace's hand to the floor and with a kick sent it spinning. He said, "My name is Gray."

"Gray?" Anne echoed bewilderedly. "Gray?" For five seconds there wasn't a sound. Then she gasped, and what burst from her lips was a questioning cry: *Alan Gray?*"

He didn't reply to her but called out, "Tomayo! Come in here! I've got this sewed up! Quit fooling with me, or I'll be out there to show you some fast shooting!"

"Eh?"

"You heard me! Bring Froke in, too, and sharp about it!"

A jeering, puzzled laugh came from Froke. "Who's givin' the orders? Who — ?"

"Me!" Gray rasped. "Who the hell d'you think is in charge here, anyhow? Me, blast you — me! *Lobo Gray of Blakeville!*"

They kept him waiting while they talked together outside the office. He overheard most of the words before they lowered their voices.

"Yes, Ned, he's the Lobo, all right."

"Why didn't you say so?"

"It might have discouraged you. His reputation . . ."

"You're too damn tricky!"

"Not a bad fellow as long as you don't cross him. I was able to get along with him, for a while . . ."

"This caper —"

"Judge Blake sent him personally . . ."

"Don't like it! What's to stop . . . burn . . ."

Gray cut in on them by stepping softly to the broken door and suddenly wrenching it wide open. The blur of their faces hung motionless in the outer radius of lamplight, turned toward him, and he could not see their hands. It was a tossup what they would do; and they watched him tensely, trying to guess his intentions.

Any attempt to placate them would be worse than useless; it would be immediately construed as a sign of weakness, and the slightest weakness now was fatal. He had to support the act of arrogantly overbearing confidence that he had launched.

"Don't play with fire, *hombres!*" he warned them, and presently two of the dimly lit faces moved slowly toward him.

Bas Tomayo entered into the office alone, on his face a curious expression that in anyone else would have passed for awe; with him, it was adulterated by mocking satire. He sauntered in, lifting a hand in half salute to Gray, nothing in his easy manner indicating that he was aware of any friction between them, past or present. Ned Froke, on his part, came only as far as the open door, and his men stayed back out of sight.

"Neat work!" Tomayo complimented Gray blandly. "You tossed back the money, and your gamble paid off, eh? I should have guessed what you were up to, but you fooled me. *Hombre de armas tomar!* I take off my hat to you, Lobo Gray!" He swept off his hat with a jaunty flourish. "We win the money *and* Mr. Wallace, as we set out to do!"

Gray said roughly, " 'We'? You and I split

up, Tomayo! Remember? I pulled this on my own!"

Since divulging his identity, he had avoided looking at Anne, and she had not uttered a sound. He did not want to look at her and see her eyes. Not ever again.

Now, at his brutally spoken claim, he heard her whisper in stunned dread, "Lobo Gray? Oh, God! No, no!" Then she was sobbing in Russell Wallace's arms, agonized sobs of racking woe and despair, and Wallace was making raging sounds deep in his throat.

Ignoring them, Tomayo smiled at Gray. "True, I did resign as your helper," he conceded. "I resigned because of what I took to be your, ah, changeable attitude. I did not resign from the game!"

"The game's closed!"

"You mean that you went at it all out for yourself and won. But my efforts have not been negligible in bringing about this happy conclusion, and therefore I say *we* have Wallace and the money!" Tomayo's spurious smile brightened. "Shall we proceed on those terms?"

Ned Froke, glowering distrustfully in the doorway, demanded, "How about me? I'm in it, too, an' I want my cut! Where's all the money you're talkin' about? We'll start with that!"

"I reckon we won't!" Gray barked. "That's mine!"

Froke narrowed his eyes. "I'll take Wallace, then! He's worth —"

"The blazes you will! I contracted to catch and deliver him alive to the Judge, and no downgrade brush-jumper gets in my way!"

He couldn't make it all stick, Gray knew. The best he could do was to aim high, then strike a deal. In this quarrel over the spoils, he stood alone against eight men, six of them skulking outside in the dark with their guns ready and the means prepared to set fire to the place at an instant's notice.

To sway Bas Tomayo back over onto his side was good trading policy at the moment, so Gray said to Froke, "It was me got this job done, with a lift from Tomayo. We didn't get any help from you. Fact is, you damn near queered it!"

"He is right, Ned," Tomayo seconded him. "Still, we do not intend to freeze you out, don't worry."

Froke gently twisted his injured forearm while looking speculatively at Gray. "I don't fall much for that kind of cackle," he objected. His eyes shifted, attracted by the shimmer of Anne's bracelet, and he sidled into the office, muttering, "Now there's a pretty li'l keepsake . . ."

Anne, chalk white, shrank from him, and Russell Wallace crouched to fight bare-handed. Gray tilted a gun, but it was Tomayo who, glancing at Gray, said, "The bauble is not worth a bullet, Ned! Better not touch the lady!"

"Huh? You mean we leave her here?"

"Hardly! She has seen and heard too much, unfortunately for her. But that is Gray's problem. You would be wise to leave her alone!"

That frustration was the last straw for Ned Froke. He backed to the door, cursing, and swung a glare at Gray.

"All right!" he roared. "All right, you're Lobo Gray! Yeah! Mister, you could be the ring-tailed ramrod o' hell, but you don't rook ol' Ned! I got six good salty jiggers there outside. They ain't schoolmarms! Nor me!"

"Nobody's trying to rook you," said Tomayo.

"Nobody's goin' to!" Froke swore. "We're taking them two an' the money down to Blakeville — all of us together, see? Let the Judge figger out what my rightful cut is; I'll 'bide by what he says. That's fair, an' it's my last word, an' be damned to you! I ain't never yet been skeered of a fight, any time, any place, an' I don't know how to bluff! Not ol' Ned!"

Tomayo murmured soothingly, "Cool off, Ned, there is no fight about that. Is there, Gray? We all go together, eh!"

It didn't suit Gray at all, and his shrug was noncommittal, but he knew that the deal was slipping out of his control and that Tomayo, acting the part of peacemaker, was in fact baring his teeth. Boxed in here, gunplay spelled swift slaughter all around, with Anne and Russell Wallace caught in the midst of it. In his flaming mood, Froke was recklessly ready to set it off, banking on his men to follow through.

Tomayo made known which side he favored by saying to Froke, "We need you, Ned, in case of trouble on the way down to Blakeville. Nobody must see us, or see who is with us, so after we set fire to this place we had better take a roundabout route and hide our tracks. You know the country —"

"Like I know my hand!"

"Then it is settled! Right, Gray?"

"It'll do," Gray said shortly. It had to be that way, a pact among robbers squabbling over the loot, a compromise to avoid a disastrous shoot-out. "Bring up the horses."

"The money!" Ned Froke grated. With his

matted beard, and the dirty blue bandanna tied over his head, he looked ferociously piratical. Gone was the cool humor he had affected earlier in the evening. Greed and ugly temper flared in his bloodshot eyes. He would not be balked. "Where's the money?"

A man outside sloshed coal oil at the little building.

Tomayo said, "Tell them to take care, Ned. I have no wish to roast before my time."

Froke, safely near the open door, rolled a heavy shoulder. "You'd be hot chili, that's sure. The money, dammit — who's got the money?"

Tomayo slid his yellow eyes to Gray. "Well?"

16
NINE KNAVES

Gray went to the safe. He unlocked it, using the key which Anne had trustingly given into his keeping, and pulled open the bulky door.

"Are you still watching my back for the judge?" he asked Tomayo and received a prompt answer:

"Never so closely as now!"

"I believe you. Your job shouldn't last much longer. What then, friend Bas?"

"Europe."

"I doubt that it's worth it."

Gray took the cashbox out of the safe. Froke laid a hungry stare on it, then swiveled a quick glance at Tomayo, who met his eyes with a look of demure amusement in which lurked a hint of inquiry. Gray saw the silent exchange. Tucking the box under his left arm, leaving his right hand free, he slammed the safe shut with his foot. He spoke to Anne and Russell Wallace without looking at them.

"Bear in mind you're under my charge. Mine, till we get where we're going. Understand? You'll do as I tell you, and you'll have to trust me not to —"

"I would as soon trust a — a rabid wolf!" breathed Anne. "A wolf is what you are, Lobo Gray! Well named! A treacherous, murdering —"

Russell Wallace gripped her arm, stilling her. The swollen veins in his narrow, austere face betrayed the rage straining within him, but when he spoke, his voice came on an even pitch. He said, "I don't fear Judge Blake or any devilish thing the scoundrel can do to me. No, I'm not afraid for myself. But Anne . . . Gray, you're a gunman, the type I condemn as a cancerous sore on the West. A professional gunman, in Judge Blake's pay — to me, nothing could be worse! But I can't believe you're totally conscienceless. I've talked with you. You've been a better man, earlier in your life. You know Blakeville — nobody knows it better! You know it's a bad place for Anne, and how bad it can be! You know!"

"I know," Gray said tonelessly. He motioned for them to precede him out of the office. "Do as I tell you!" he said, and they walked by him, passing between him and Ira Hamp's body on the floor. Tomayo went on out, too, but Froke paused to pick up the dead man's hat. Ira Hamp was due to be cremated; he wouldn't need his hat. It didn't fit Froke, though, and he flung it down again.

They gathered under the tall old cottonwoods, waiting, but not for long. Saddled horses were brought up: uncurried animals belonging to Froke and his men; mounts from the corrals for Anne and Russell Wallace; Gray's and Tomayo's borrowed Twin Peaks horses; and several purloined spares for the road.

Last to mount, Gray looked the party over. He was in charge, he had stated, and he meant to make it stick if he could. Gun prestige — that was all that upheld his tenuous rule over the Froke gang. He knew their kind. Sullen, mutinous, like savages, eager to pounce on any self-elected leader at the first show of weakness, they recognized only the brute right of force and violence. Brush-jumpers.

"They love you not, Lobo Gray!" murmured Bas Tomayo maliciously beside him. "They do not forget or forgive how you drove them out of the house! Nothing is forgiven!"

Gray narrowed a glance at him. "How about you?"

Tomayo giggled. "Really, now, you ought to know me by now. I am not affected by petty resentment."

"No?"

"Not when so much money is at stake. My love of money outbalances all other emotions. When I kill for it, I kill without personal feeling. It is always best, otherwise one may give way to a premature impulse . . ."

Gray tied up the cashbox with a latigo and strung it securely on his saddle horn.

"O.K., if we're ready to go!" he announced, ranging a stare over the hard, hairy faces in the moonlight. "Let's not crowd together. String out. Wallace and his

213

sister ride up front with me. They'll be out o' your dust — and out o' the blackmouth you spill so free. Tomayo —"

"I'll ride ahead with Ned," Tomayo interrupted blandly. "He knows the country. But I'll keep in touch with you, so you won't go astray in the dark." Common idiom occasionally crept into his precise fashion of speaking. He said, "Let's go!" and flipped a lighted match at the oil-soaked front of the office.

They got going in that order: Ned Froke leading the way with Tomayo, Gray following with Anne and Russell Wallace, the six men of the gang bringing up the rear. The arrangement wasn't good, from Gray's viewpoint, but it was a natural one, difficult to argue against. Bas Tomayo had a knack for offering perfectly logical suggestions that covered every contingency. Friend Bas, mused Gray bleakly, was literally and figuratively a little bastard.

Gray looked back once at the house and outbuildings of Twin Peaks. The burning office made a flickering patch of yellow, brightening rapidly in the moonlit black and gray of its surroundings, beginning to cast a high glare up into the cottonwoods. He saw that Anne was also looking back. Her lips moved. She was praying, he guessed. Or

214

maybe she was saying farewell forever to Twin Peaks. Like himself.

Like himself; lost and gone.

Morning sunlight found them traveling dead south, closely following the river. They had pursued a circuitous course out and away from the Sierra Verde, taking most of the night. Their horses were no longer fresh, and the tight order of travel had loosened. It had been agreed that the open trail by daylight presented too great a risk of their being sighted and reported, so they stayed clear of it. They rode along under the cover of the high bank cut by past floods and left dry when the river had shifted its sandy course. Hills, shelving upward beyond the winding line of high cutbank, gave them still further protection. Screened from sight, like wary bobcats avoiding the skyline, they worked their way steadily down toward Blakeville.

Leading, but from settled habit glancing backward every so often, Tomayo and Froke had let their horses slacken to a walk, to conserve them, for there yet remained far to go. Fifty yards behind Gray, Anne, and Russell Wallace, Froke's six men rode in a bunch, smoking and yawning, slouched in their saddles. Boredom and loss of sleep had not dulled their underlying alertness. Their eyes were never still.

Anne rode with head bowed, as if half asleep or sunk in apathy, but Russell Wallace, erect, stared straight ahead, too icily proud to show the slightest sign of weariness or despair. They stayed half a horse's length in advance of Gray, had kept to that distance from him ever since leaving Twin Peaks, and not one word had passed among them.

As the sun rose higher and the harsh heat of the day pressed down, Tomayo looked backward more often. At last, with a sudden restlessness unusual in him, he reined his horse sharply about, said something to Froke, and came riding back at a canter. He nodded to Gray in passing and, ignoring Anne and Wallace, joined the six men in the rear. Presently he left them and came up behind Gray.

"We will not reach Blakeville until after dark at this rate, eh?"

The question was an idle one. He could estimate the distance and rate of travel as well as anybody. Gray glanced around at him and saw that he was frowning with a strange irritation.

"Yeah. Late tonight, if nothing stops us."

Tomayo's frown deepened. The frown

wiped all the effeminate quality from his dark face and left it sullenly saturnine.

"Well — plenty of time," he muttered obscurely. He rode in pace with Gray for another minute, then abruptly put spurs to his horse and rejoined Froke up forward.

Gray watched him go and let his eyes drift elsewhere. The false riverbed stretched on southward like a wide, sunken road, its wind-rippled sand untrodden, broken only by silvery green clumps of chamiso, the sky a hard, clean blue above it. In this lonely land, all colors were bleached; everything was a pale flash in the sunlight, in the silence, and shadows had no depth.

On his right, the eroded cutbank and overlooking hills passed by slowly, changing their shapes, yet retaining always their monotonous sameness. Here and there, where the hills folded, dry arroyos gashed the bank to debouch onto the flat riverbed, most of them short and narrow, like cramped alleys opening into a main street. The hot sun climbed toward noon, eating away the depthless shadows.

He laid a thorough regard on the mouth of the arroyo which Tomayo and Froke ahead were riding past. The arroyo, he judged from the contour of the several hills that folded together above it, was what

Mexicans called an *arroyo madre* — a mother arroyo, fed by many smaller ones. Its mouth made a deep gap in the bank where, in the rare times of heavy rain, it spewed forth torrents, although now it was dust dry. Almost certainly its crooked length extended all the way up into the jumble of hills.

He looked behind. The six men were guffawing over something that apparently had to do with Bas Tomayo, and Gray's look was casually interested, as if he wouldn't mind sharing the joke. They were enlarging on it with snickering comments, making it do lengthy service in driving out their boredom. Gray faced front again. He spoke quietly to Anne and Wallace.

"Listen!" he said. "I've got something to say to you!" They ignored him, and he had to repeat it, adding, "It won't keep! There's less than a minute left!"

Anne scarcely moved her head. "Say it, then! We can't stop you, can we? Any more than we can stop you from —"

"Shut up!" Gray said. "Shut up and hear me! Wallace, we were trapped tight last night at Twin Peaks. You didn't have a chance. I did what I had to do. It was better than us burning alive, or having them go hog wild . . ."

Russell Wallace snorted derisively. "Why trouble to make excuses for yourself? You're Lobo Gray. That name is familiar to all of us. You came up from Blakeville to get me for Judge Blake, for blood money, and you've succeeded. Nothing you say can alter that! I'm not a complete fool!"

"Maybe I'm the fool," Gray said. "Or maybe it's because I was once called Alan. Or because —"

"Alan!" Anne whispered, and now her head came up. "You *are* — you really are — !"

"Wallace," Gray said, "you see this arroyo we're coming to. You and Anne turn off there when I give the word. Ride up it and keep going, fast as your horses can go. Here, take your cashbox with you. The money's all in it, not a dollar short. I don't owe you a damn thing!"

"What? What d'you mean?"

"You heard me. Do as I tell you. Ready, now!"

Anne and Russell Wallace looked at him, seeing the same scarred and battered face, the same hard mouth. If there was any difference, it was only that the underlying sadness in the eyes was more pronounced, and even that was leavened by a kind of serene resignation.

Wallace exclaimed unbelievingly, "Are you telling us to escape — make a run for it? Impossible!"

"What's impossible about it?"

"Froke — Tomayo — the others — !"

"I figure to hold 'em back long enough for you two to get a fair start," Gray said almost tranquilly. "I'm a gunman, remember. Fight's my game; has been for years."

"Alan — !"

"The pony preacher who married us, I gave him all the money I had. Dollar and six bits. Figured it was worth it. All right, here's your arroyo. Get going!"

"Alan! You can't — !"

"The hell I can't!"

He hauled his mount around broadside to them, crowding them both into the mouth of the *arroyo madre.* He booted their dancing horses and snatched off his hat and slapped them with it. They took off, and he watched them go plunging strongly up the curving course of the arroyo. He smiled, feeling a joyous relief.

He saw them both look back just before they met the first bend and rounded it out of his sight. Anne's raven hair was flying over her neck and shoulders. Her lips parted, and she called back to him, but he couldn't hear her words above the stamp and slither of climbing hoofs. He waved after her and laughed easily for the first time in years. By God, there went a woman. He had not hunted a mirage, those years, no. A woman. The years were not wasted.

A babble of shouting had burst out. The six men in the rear dropped their paltry joke and spurred their horses forward. Froke and Tomayo whirled about, digging at their holsters, Froke cursing and Tomayo ejaculating clearly, "Judas!"

Gray said aloud, "I'm Lobo Gray of Blakeville, and this is my day!" He slid off his horse and slapped it farewell, and the animal, balking at climbing the arroyo, trotted snorting out into the open.

He spread his shoulders and took a deep breath, drew his guns, and cast a look up at the sky. Shining blue, the sky was, unflawed, clean as a baby's conscience.

"What a day!" he said and laughed again.

It wasn't so bad to end this way, a day like this. Not so bad at all. Better by far than that grubby alley in Trail Fork. He knew his enemies here. He knew what he was fighting for.

17
GRAY'S FOLLY

Gray fired twice. He fired from the mouth of the arroyo as the six rear-guard men, first to come up, swirled into his vision. Two of them spilled, bumping awkwardly from their saddles and striking the ground head and shoulders foremost. They ruled out any misunderstanding, and the remaining four swerved in close to the cutbank. They piled off their horses and cautiously changed tactics . . . but not too cautiously. Violence was natural to them, and it could never catch them unready, but two shots and two down added up to a thoughtful score.

Charging up from the opposite direction with Tomayo, Ned Froke shouted urgently, "Get 'im, dammit, get 'im! Them two are gettin' away! What the hell — !"

His bull nerve did not desert him. He came charging straight on. The blue sheen of his gun barrel shortened to a pinpoint as Gray swung his smoking guns. Froke had the full use of only one arm. His wounded left arm was swollen and discolored, and his eyes were feverish.

He triggered a single shot hurriedly, hooked his reins, and wrenched his horse up rearing. His hairy head hunched down, and the horse took Gray's bullet. The horse floundered and crashed into Tomayo riding alongside.

On the left, the four men eased around a shoulder of the cutbank. The first of them got off a shot that sent Gray's hat spinning, and Gray had to pull back, affording Froke and Tomayo their opportunity to get themselves unscrambled.

Gray backed up into the arroyo and stood fast, waiting for the next move. Nothing stirred. A baffling silence closed down. The sounds of the two horses carrying Anne and Wallace to safety grew fainter and died away. He speculated about the doings now of Tomayo and Froke and the four men, until he heard scrambling noises and grasped their ominous meaning.

"Might've known it!" he muttered.

Storming the mouth of the arroyo wasn't good, they had found, so they began climbing up the cutbank on foot to get above the arroyo and shoot down at him. That was their best play, much as it infuriated them to leave their horses and expend precious time while Anne and Wallace escaped.

With difficulty, Gray clambered up the left side of the arroyo, clawing his fingers into the sand, and got to where he could peer over the edge. Two of the men had reached the higher ground and were running across it, angling toward the arroyo and motioning to somebody over on its north side. One of them spied the bandage on Gray's head and yipped a warning. Both running men dived to the ground and Gray's shot at them went wasted.

A gun rapped somewhere behind Gray. Sand exploded near his face. His instinctive jerk cost him his grip, and he tumbled to the bottom in a shower of rubble.

"I got 'im!" bellowed Froke. "Close in on him, quick!"

"Go easy, Ned!" Tomayo sang out. "He's hard to kill!"

"Not for me! Not for ol' Ned, he ain't!"

A blue bandanna and bearded face bulged into sight above the south edge of the arroyo. Gray sliced a gun up and fired. The face vanished.

"Right in the whiskers!" commented Tomayo. "You'll never look the same, Ned! He's a shooting fool. Can't say I didn't warn you, can you?"

Froke could be heard cursing him. At the end of a string of oaths, he snarled, "Do some shootin' y'self, you goddam yaller-eyed scutter, or are you skeered of 'im?"

Silence fell once more. Gray listened

intently for the coming of the four on the north and Tomayo on the south, knowing that they were creeping over the higher ground to the arroyo. Once they reached it he would be without cover, vulnerable as a bear trapped in a pit. There was nothing left for him to do but wait, using up the shrinking margin of his time, watching for them to show themselves for that fleet instant that it would take them to shoot.

Something moved stealthily along the north edge. A long pause, and the peak of a hat shyly rose an inch. Gray slung a shot at it. The hat spun away.

Four gun muzzles poked immediately into view from four different points, on the north edge. A fifth muzzle, on the south edge, covered him, behind it a blue bandanna and a bearded, bloodied face. He had fallen for the hoary old hat trick, because it was so stale he didn't think anyone would seriously use it on him. He was located and nailed on the spot.

"Let me have 'im, boys!" said Froke.

A gun roared muffledly. Froke uttered a harsh cry, and his thick body reared up, twisting, his gun weaving. There was another report, and Gray, about to fire, saved a shell. Froke was falling. A thud, and the outlaw hit the edge. His legs went up, outweighed by his torso, and he slid head first into the arroyo.

The four gun muzzles lining the north edge were silent and motionless, as though their owners had received a shocking surprise that momentarily rendered them incapable of action. Then they snapped up, all four in unison, leveled out and spurting.

Bas Tomayo appeared suddenly. He must have sprung quickly to his feet, from lying prostrate behind Froke, but now he was walking, unhurried and short-stepped. He was smiling his shallow smile over a pair of blaring guns.

Gray saved another bullet, one intended for Tomayo. He took the bead off him at the last instant, for Tomayo was shooting straight across the arroyo, not down at him, and the four men on the other side were blazing back at Tomayo. Gray couldn't see the four now; only the puffs of their guns. They were falling back. Tomayo came on.

His dapper little figure jerked slightly, and he broke stride. A stone might have rolled under his foot. Recovering his balance, he concentrated calmly on the four. Only his lips smiled. His yellow eyes were wide open, their gaze as hypnotic as the fixed stare of a madman.

The furious gun battle lasted a brief moment and ceased abruptly, as though a door were slammed shut on it. While its echoes still grumbled in the hills and footsteps stumbled faintly in retreat, Tomayo advanced one more pace to the arroyo and stepped blindly over the edge with his guns held forward.

Gray caught him with outstretched arms. It was like catching a falling boy, a slender boy of perhaps twelve or fourteen, he was so light; yet his body was of steel and perfectly proportioned in the form of a man in miniature. Gray laid him down on the sandy floor.

Tomayo's silk shirt showed two round dots that rapidly enlarged to dark wet blotches and merged together. The little man could not quite focus his eyes, but he was able to pronounce distinctly and with emphasis, "Mr. Gray, you *are* a fool!"

"*Señor* Tomayo, you're another!" said Gray.

Hoofs stamped a confused pattern of running, and a flurry of horses swept past the mouth of the arroyo. One of Froke's men had got away. True to his trade of horse thief, he was taking all the horses with him.

Evidently hardly conscious of the temporary commotion, Tomayo quirked his lips wryly. "Two of us. Should have been one.

Only one. You. Something went wrong . . ."

The sounds of the running horses beat low and faded out, and the vast silence of the lonely land closed down all around.

"What got into you, friend Bas? I figured you were on their side. I'd have sworn you were out to kill me."

Tomayo smiled, rolling his head on the ground. "You were only half right. My private bargain with His Honor was explicit. Help you get the job done, but don't let you come back alive. Two birds with one stone. Capture Wallace — and get rid of a dangerously uncontrollable ramrod who knows too much."

"I guessed that, finally."

"Yes. I thought about shooting you in the back this morning. But I knew you would play some crazy trick today, and I decided to wait for it. Let you fight it out with Froke and his animals. I would finish it. Win everything for myself."

The cold-bloodedness of it moved Gray to say, "You meant to murder whoever was left — Froke, any of his men, or me! For the cashbox, and the bounty on Wallace, and —"

"Why not?" Tomayo closed his eyes wearily, as if dismissing an obvious conclusion. "I have killed for much less . . . big men especially. In a way, you epitomize those big men who all my life have sneered at my littleness, my ineradicably dainty manners and little graces, my freakish looks . . ."

"Why didn't you go through with it, then?" Gray asked him. "What went wrong?"

Tomayo gave a small shrug, then winced. He opened his eyes. "I got into the fight too soon. I meant to wait, I swear, and settle whoever was left. But Wallace and Anne were getting away fast, with the cashbox. And then it came to me again that you — that you — no matter how angry, you have never spoken to me as if I were — well, different. Less than a man. Nor even looked at me in that way. No, not even when you shoved a gun in my face. That doesn't mean a thing to you, does it?"

"No."

"It does to me. I tried to prod you into saying something that would make it easy for me to hate you — I actually did, several times. Most of us are capable of hating, and we can accept hatred, but we can't bear ridicule because it cuts too deeply. It cuts open a man's ego and lays bare his secret insufficiencies, and that is intolerable. Yes, I have killed for it, friend Gray."

"Like you killed Froke," Gray said.

"Shot him in the back. Easy — after what he called me. Easier than not shooting you while I had the chance. That has cost me everything. Damned foolish of me. I shall never see Europe again." Tomayo moved his right hand, and Gray clasped it. "Damned fools — both of us — each in his own way, eh?"

"Could call us that," Gray said.

Tomayo chuckled faintly. "You doubt it? We each had the world by the tail . . . and we let it go. . . ." His small fingers in Gray's big hand twitched and fell limp.

After a while, Gray stood up. The crunch of his heels in the sand made the only sound in the quietness. He looked down at Tomayo and said, "I'll push on to Blakeville and see the Judge. Might's well go through with the damn foolishness, *amigo,* huh? Tough on foot, but I might's well."

He was talking to himself. Tomayo was dead. Gray left the silent arroyo, taking Tomayo's guns with him.

The horses were gone, and he turned right and limped southward. Back to Blakeville. Back where he had started from, to face the Judge. It was going to be a long, tough trek on foot with a lame leg, but he guessed he could finish this last task if he kept his mind on Anne and Wallace and on the good future that was possible for them at Twin Peaks if nothing intervened . . . if he kept in mind that he was Lobo Gray, who should have died decently as Alan Gray years ago in the war.

The effort would occupy him and serve to lay the ghosts, drive out the haunting black imps. And at the end of the trek, he would find rest.

18
THE LAST OF LOBO GRAY

In the midafternoon's scorching heat, the main street of Blakeville slumbered undisturbed by Gray's plodding arrival. The somnolence extended even to the Bullhead Bar and to Paley's Palace opposite, two establishments that rarely knew silence. Or so it appeared until inspection picked out the details of shadowy faces behind windows and stony-eyed men shading in doorways. All men. Some females lived in Blakeville, and a few children; no ladies. Today, women and children stayed out of sight, not because of the heat. Blakeville was "Anglo" in the Southwestern sense and did not subscribe to the sensible Spanish custom of siesta.

Gray trudged on, slowly and steadily, each

step a painful exertion, to the imposing white house on the low hill overlooking the town. Nobody paid him greeting, and the men in doorways withheld all sign of recognition. They looked at him as if seeing an unwanted stranger in the gaunt man with the bad limp who shambled by on broken boots. Then they looked through him; and he had the feeling that he was invisible, or that his mind was playing tricks and he would come to in a minute and find himself still on the trail down. That interminable, infernal trail; resting wherever he fell when his leg gave out, coming awake with a start, chilled at night, baked by day, ants crawling through his sweat-sour clothes. Three days.

He stumbled, climbing the steps of the white house, and in rocking hard onto his bad leg he suffered the ignominy of falling to his knees. At the front door, two house guards quietly materialized, one on either side of him. They wore the round metal badges of special deputies — hand-picked enforcers. Not long ago, they had taken their orders from him. Now they plucked the guns from his holsters and without a word motioned for him to go on in, and he was too spent to care about it. He was weak with starvation. He couldn't recall when he had last eaten, yet the thought of food turned his stomach. A taste of copper filled his mouth. The smell in his nostrils was his own stale smell, and he thought dully, I stink; I stink like a dead skunk. . . .

Judge Blake sat in his oversize swivel chair behind his big, untidy desk, the air above him blue with cigar smoke, his relaxed manner conveying the impression that Gray's arrival was not only expected but welcomed as a relief from stern official duties.

"Ah, there, Gray!"

He chose at first not to show any notice that Gray was a ragged scarecrow whose haggard face looked ghastly ill beneath the dirty head bandage. Gray halted before the desk and stood shakily on one leg. His head throbbed. He had trouble adjusting his inflamed eyes to the shadow of the office, after the days in the sun, and he moistened his throat with difficulty.

" 'Lo, Judge," he croaked.

"Sit down, Gray."

Gray sat down. This time, he thought. *This time!*

He guessed that his slow approach had been sighted and reported before he entered town. The Judge had made ready for him this time. And the house guards, the special deputies, the enforcers. Blakeville was ready.

He was not supposed to have come back alive.

Well, I'm not much more than half alive, at that, he thought. He stared dully at the Judge.

The same strong face, heavy jowls, bald, Romanlike head. Same overwhelming presence and ponderous dignity, buttered with professional charm and honeyed with condescension. The Judge glanced over his desk down at Gray's ruined boots and in his full, round voice inquired, "Been walking?"

"Yeah," Gray said.

He rested back in the chair. A wave of nausea rose in him. He compressed his cracked lips and fought it down. It was unbearably stuffy in this room. He sweated. The sweat was clammy cold under his armpits and on his forehead. The tendons of his hard-used leg tightened, and nerves crawled and twitched all along its length. The leg was stiffening quickly again, because he was seated, but he hadn't the energy left to rise.

"How did you make out up there?" he heard the Judge ask him.

He muttered back, "Don't you know?"

"One of Froke's men turned up here with some horses two days ago. He was hurt, and he talked wild. I want the story from you,

Gray." The Judge spoke almost with indifference, but the shine was hot in his eyes. "How did you make out?"

"*Bueno*," Gray answered. "Some trouble, but we handled it, Tomayo and me. Froke got in on it. We learned all their plans. We captured Wallace. And the war chest . . ."

"*Bueno* is right!"

"And — Wallace's sister. Did you know about her?"

"Anne Wallace?" murmured the Judge. "Of course. She's half owner of Twin Peaks. She was born there."

"How's that?" Gray sat upright. "It's impossible! She's a Texan born and raised!"

The Judge gazed at him. "Sometimes," he said, "a thing does seem impossible on the face of it. The Froke man, for instance, told a wild tale of you deliberately letting the Wallaces escape with their war chest. And of Tomayo turning his guns on Froke. Incredible!"

"You can start believing it!"

Thick silence ran for a full minute. The Judge forgot to smoke, holding his cigar suspended inches from his pursed lips. Gray eased his leg out straight. He wasn't sweating anymore, nor shaking, and he said:

"Don Basilio Tomayo went under. He took Froke and three of his men with him, after

I helped the Wallaces make a run for it. You picked the right man for my back-watcher, but he was the wrong man to put a bullet in my back when we got the job done. Yeah — it was *bueno* to hell, Judge, how we made out up there!"

The Judge shortened his gaze to his cigar. It had gone out, and he dropped it. "You let them go. And the money. You and Tomayo." He spoke musingly. "Discouraging, how a man's best plans can be smashed by a human quirk. The enemy of progress, I sometimes think, is human nature itself. I've felt unsure of you from the very first, Gray. You've helped me build up what I have —"

"I wish I could see it torn down!"

"I know." The Judge nodded absently, as at a side remark having only a minor bearing on his main train of thought. "You're the kind of man who has to go all the way, once your mind is made up. No — not your mind; your heart. That's what makes you so dangerous, yet so vulnerable to a man who is guided exclusively by his intelligence, as I am. I could easily have had you shot down before you got here, you know."

"I figured you wouldn't."

"That was close figuring. I wanted the truth about what had happened to Wallace, and knew I'd get it from you, of course."

The Judge's eyes flared, then chilled to sharp perception and fixed on Gray's face. "What else did you figure?"

A sullen rumble grew audible, like the sustained growl of an approaching thunderstorm, sending a commotion through the town, the sounds mingling, muffled by the thick walls of the big house. In the hushed room, the swivel chair creaked, the Judge reaching forward to his row of desk drawers.

"Let's have a smoke, Gray . . ."

"That's the wrong drawer, Judge!"

"It's the right one for this brand of smoke!" said the Judge, lifting a pistol from the drawer and firing over the desk.

Although Gray was lunging aside out of his chair as the pistol came up, the point-blank discharge could not miss him. Burned powder stung his right cheek and eye, and the bullet ripped like the slash of a hot knife along the muscles of his neck. The Judge fired at his face, suddenly surmising that he was not entirely disarmed, that something had escaped the eyes of the house guards.

Underneath his shirt, Tomayo's pair of guns lay flat in the starved hollow of Gray's stomach, held by the belt of his pants, and he tore his shirt open with both hands, rooting them out. Their front sights gouged his stomach at the beltline, and he shot as soon as he got them clear, for the Judge was cocking the pistol while bringing it to bear on him again.

Too fast. His vision was blurred. A clumsy heaviness roughened the co-ordination of his muscles and nerves. Both of his bullets whipped papers stacked loosely on the desk. One, deflected, nicked the Judge and caused him to flinch and thereby spoil his shot, his thumb slipping off the hammer while it was yet at half cock, letting it slap down on the empty shell. For an instant, he and Gray glared at each other.

The muffled rumble had become a solid drumming that gathered further noises, swelling to a confused uproar. All Blakeville seemed to be swiftly drawn into it.

The door burst open, exposing the staring face of one of the house guards. Hurriedly cocking the pistol, the Judge flinched again, his chill nerves disturbed. The house guard shouted urgently, "Judge — !" Then, seeing that Gray was armed, he brought up the gun that he carried in his hand.

Gray forced his muscles to obedience and worked each of his trigger fingers twice. The four fast reports crashed a deafening chatter in the room. Two for the Judge and two for the house guard, who fired into the floor in the act of falling forward.

The Judge had not risen from his oversize swivel chair. It groaned under his shifting weight, and the cocked pistol scraped across the surface of the desk. Rage at last shrank his eyes to muddy little pools, smeared the bogus nobility of his face, and all at once he was a bloated old man mouthing gutter obscenities in a strangled whine. In what seemed curiously like a fit of peevish spite, he squeezed a shot from the pistol in his hand lying on the desk as his bald head sank over it. The shot scored a burn- and splinter-fringed track in the desk top, straight at Gray.

Gray groped for the chair that he had vacated and slumped into it. He rested his guns on his knees; they were so heavy he could barely manage to hold them. Through sluggish swirls of thickening mist, he watched the door. The house guard he had shot lay half in, half out, inert. Others should be coming on the run. It was getting noisier outside, everybody shouting. Sounded like election day in Chihuahua, that time when . . .

A stammering volley of gunfire roused him. He took a deep breath to clear his head, and powder smoke acridly filled his lungs and brought on a coughing spell that ended when the tingling in his nostrils made him sneeze.

The sneeze shook him to pieces. It exploded the top of his head off. His eyeballs jumped out. He heard the two thumps of them on the floor, and he reached his empty hands down to recover them, but then the dark mist broke up into millions of bright fragments. The fragments were sliver-sharp, cutting into him, and he was floating among them and being sliced into careful little bits.

Time slowly began again, measured by a hammer pounding him in maniacal rhythm with his heartbeats. He was arguing with someone.

"She couldn't have been born at Twin Peaks. Her folks were the Provosts, who bought the place next to ours down on the Nueces when she was a little toddler. Came from Dallas. They didn't think too much of me later on, 'count of my old man. That's why we got married in secret. Her name's Gray by right, not Wallace . . ."

He thought he was saying this in argument. But his mouth was shut tight, and presently he realized that he was making sounds like querulous moaning behind clenched teeth, and next he became conscious of lying in a moving vehicle. Traffic noises beat at his ears: jingling harness, creaking saddles, clatter of hoofs, and an undertone of men's voices — the disciplined hubbub of many horsemen and wheeled rigs all traveling in the same direction.

"He sounds too hurt to go on," someone said.

"No, I'm not," Gray mumbled. "It's not that. I just want to know . . ."

The one who had spoken raised a shout of command. The whole column of traffic shuffled to a standstill. Gray dragged open his eyelids and stared in astonishment at the hawk face of Russell Wallace. He strove to sit up.

He was lying in a surrey, one of Judge Blake's fancy rigs; the back seat had been knocked out to convert it into a traveling litter for him. On the trail behind were various other rigs, with bands of armed horsemen flanking them and riding rear guard. The horsemen had tired faces, and the rigs carried wounded men, but all looked grimly cheerful.

Wallace placed a hand on Gray's chest and with surprising gentleness forced him back down. "Take it easy, now! We've got to get you home in one piece. Don't worry yourself about Blakeville. Or the Judge. You put the finish to him for good, and we —"

"I want to know —" Gray began again.

"I'm telling you," Wallace said patiently. "These men are my vigilantes, so don't look wall-eyed at them. Damned fine company of men. Texans, mostly. With Texas on her side, I swear it's hard to see how the South lost the war. I rode hard to the camp and got them. Anne went with me. Coming down, we stopped at that arroyo — to bury you, I thought, but your boot tracks wobbled south out of it. Seven dead men lying around there."

"Tomayo sided with me. He ought to have decent burial. But I want to know —"

"It shall be done. I sent Anne back home from there. She was worn out and dead for sleep, but she gave me the devil. I had to put my foot down!" Wallace cleared his throat. "That is," he amended, "I talked her into going back for Marley and the rest. Told her we absolutely needed them. Anything to get her out of the way, with a fight in view. And it was a fight, a right smart fight. These Lone Star larrupers know how. We took Blakeville like Grant took . . . gr-rr-*hum!* Pity you missed it."

"I was — doing something else."

"So we found! We can expect troublesome repercussions from our doings, of course. Official repercussions, civil and military.

242

But" — Wallace raised a bony forefinger — "there will be no scapegoats! They'd have to arrest every man in the Sierra Verde, because we all share the responsibility, and it's our habit to stick together. And you're a Sierra Verde man now, branded and earmarked, regardless of — ah — any and all previous conditions of service, as the Army phrase goes."

"But I want to know —"

"Your place is at Twin Peaks. I'm a pretty fair ranch manager. I have a head for business. Frankly, though, I'm not a good foreman. Neither was Hamp, come to think of it, for all his push and hustle. What is it you want to know?"

"Where was Anne born?"

Wallace blinked, taken aback by the unexpected irrelevance of Gray's query, but he answered promptly, "Twin Peaks."

"No," Gray said, "she wasn't. I mean Anne, my wife."

Along the halted column, horses drooped their heads and stood three-legged, riders lounged bow-backed in their saddles, and drivers of the commandeered rigs from Blakeville passed canteens and flasks among the wounded. The river on the right of the trail, struck by the slanting sun, was a golden streak.

Wallace arched his eyebrows at Gray. "I know perfectly well who you mean," he retorted dryly; "Anne, my sister." Then, reading Gray's expression, he frowned forbiddingly, and quick comprehension flickered in his eyes. He said, "If you were anybody else, anybody but my brother-in-law — and if you weren't as damaged as you are — I'd . . ."

"You'd what?"

"I'd kick you for what you're thinking!"

"I've still got a kick left in *me!*" Gray once more attempted to rise, and again Wallace pushed him back, less gently than before.

"Stay down," Wallace said, "and hear me. Anne is my sister. *My sister!*" he repeated distinctly. "My kid sister. I was ten when she was born. At Twin Peaks! Our parents, for reasons best forgotten, broke up. My father kept me with him. My mother took Anne — she was still an infant — and soon after the divorce, she remarried. She was originally from Texas, and the man she married was a Texan. His name was Provost. For a while they lived in Dallas, then went into ranching."

"On the lower Nueces," Gray muttered.

"Down near the Mexico line, yes," Wallace said. "You know the place. You lived nearby. Anne has told me everything. I

244

never knew Provost, but apparently he was a good father to her. Brought her up as his own daughter."

"I thought she was."

"So did she, until Provost died and her mother — our mother — told her. You were in the war then. I was, too, but my father fell ill, and I pulled strings to go home and take care of him and the ranch. As it turned out, he was dying and was very angry about it. In most ways, he was quite a man." Wallace's crispness lost its edge. "He had always managed to keep track of my mother after she left him. I suppose he never really stopped caring about her. He told me he had received word that she was widowed, and he was worried for her and Anne."

He paused, and Gray said, "It's all right for you to kick me now."

Wallace nodded absently. "He was afraid for them, living down there without a man left on the place to protect them. He knew how conditions were there while the war was still going on. Indians raiding up from Mexico, practically unhindered. Bandits and renegades roaming the border. The upshot was that I went down there to see what I could do. My own mother and sister, you know. . . . As luck would have it, somebody spotted me for a Union officer, and I was taken as a spy. Damned silly — war nearly over and nothing to spy on but their god-forsaken chaparral. I got away, but when I reached the Provost place —"

"I saw it later," Gray said. "I know what you did, not how you did it. Those border Apaches couldn't have been easy."

"They had a bunch of stolen ponies. I stampeded them. Grabbed Anne before they could do her any real harm." Wallace passed it off with a shrug. "We crossed the border and followed it west. Crossed it again, and I brought her to Twin Peaks. Father was dead and buried by the time we got there."

"I didn't know who you were. Thought you must be some kind of Yankee scalawag" — Gray caught himself — "I looked for you and Anne in Mexico."

"A rumor reached us once that you had showed up at your old home after the war and disappeared the same day," Wallace mentioned. "Only a rumor, and I couldn't go back down there to look into it. Civil authorities still wanted me for shooting a couple of fellows when I broke arrest. We tried to have you traced. Tried everything. Notices are still being run in Texas papers."

"I never went back to Texas."

"Can't say I blame you for that. Nor for — other things, now that I know what's been on your mind." Wallace paused. "It seemed best for Anne to take her own name of Wallace after she came to live at Twin Peaks. If she hadn't, people would have wondered. They might even have wondered if it really was my kid sister I'd brought home from Texas. Know what I mean?"

He touched Gray lightly with the toe of his boot. "Here's that kick," he said and sprang down from the surrey. "Let's push on, if you can stand it."

Near sundown, some of the foremost riders in the moving column called out, pointing forward, "Posse!"

"Marley and the bunch," said Wallace. "The famed Sierra Verde Pool — late as a June snow!" Then he exclaimed, "By God, she's with them! Wouldn't you think she'd had enough?"

Gray got his head and shoulders up, and this time Wallace helped him. The Sierra Verde cowmen, determinedly but belatedly thundering down the river trail, checked their speed at sight of the returning column, but a single rider in the lead shot out ahead at a dead run. Bent low in the saddle, hatless, raven hair flying, the oncoming rider threw up her hand, and her voice came floating forward on a high note of desperately urgent inquiry.

Gray raised his arm. Wallace took hold of it and waved it for him in answer.

We hope you have enjoyed this Large Print book. Other Thorndike, Wheeler, and Chivers Press Large Print books are available at your library or directly from the publishers.

For information about current and upcoming titles, please call or write, without obligation, to:

Publisher
Thorndike Press
295 Kennedy Memorial Drive
Waterville, ME 04901
Tel. (800) 223-1244

or visit our Web site at:

www.gale.com/thorndike
www.gale.com/wheeler

OR

Chivers Large Print
published by BBC Audiobooks Ltd
St James House, The Square
Lower Bristol Road
Bath BA2 3SB
England
Tel. +44(0) 800 136919
email: bbcaudiobooks@bbc.co.uk
www.bbcaudiobooks.co.uk

All our Large Print titles are designed for easy reading, and all our books are made to last.